The Wild Child

Judith Bowen

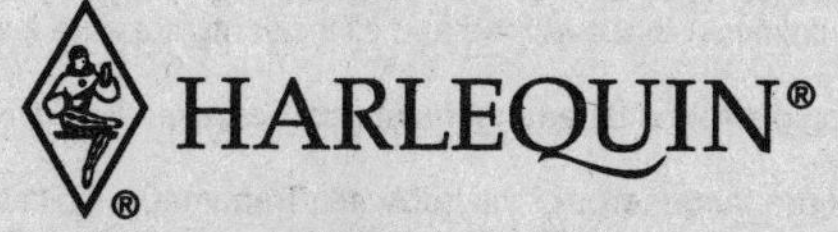

TORONTO • NEW YORK • LONDON
AMSTERDAM • PARIS • SYDNEY • HAMBURG
STOCKHOLM • ATHENS • TOKYO • MILAN • MADRID
PRAGUE • WARSAW • BUDAPEST • AUCKLAND

ISBN 0-373-71160-3

THE WILD CHILD

This edition published by arrangement with Harlequin Books S.A.

Visit us at www.eHarlequin.com

Printed in U.S.A.

"Hey!" she called to the child and the big black dog.

Eva waved her hand, smiling. "Don't worry. I won't hurt you."

The child raised one hand in a hesitant response to Eva's gesture and then slipped off the boulder. Eva stumbled forward, cursing the pebbles that hurt her feet and slowed her progress. Where were they—behind the boulder? Across the creek? Into the woods on the other side?

If not, they'd vanished into thin air again!

Eva didn't know what to do. This was just too strange. Who *was* this little kid, out yesterday and today just—just wandering! Where was the mother? The father?

"*Oh, how I love* Judith Bowen's *stories! Such gutsy heroines and such lovable men! You can't put the books down and you remember them with a fond, tender feeling.* Now, *that's romance!*"

—Bestselling author Anna Jacobs

Dear Reader,

The Sunshine Coast of British Columbia is a special place for me. My husband and I met there while I was working for the *Sechelt Press* and he was working for the *Coast News*. True love—over a village council meeting!

Liberty Island is fictitious, of course, but most of the other places and islands mentioned in *The Wild Child* are not. If you take a ferry from Horseshoe Bay today and get off at Langdale, you can meander up the rugged coast on your way to Earl's Cove, stopping at Molly's Lane and visiting the gravesite of the mysterious Danish prince at Roberts Creek. You can even poke your head in at the Half Moon Bay store and buy a loaf of bread made by the lightkeeper's wife.

Eva and Silas meet on an island peopled by ghosts—the legendary but never seen Liberty Island goats, the tangled relationships from the past, living only in dusty love letters and old jewelry now, the remembered games of happy childhood summers spent on the island.

Silas shares his life with his secret daughter now, the wild girl of Liberty Island. Eva knows where her duty lies—but can she betray Silas, the man she's come to love? I hope you enjoy Eva and Silas's story. It's a story very close to my heart.

Judith Bowen

P.S. Write to me at P.O. Box 2333, Point Roberts, WA 98281-2333 or visit me at www.judithbowen.com.

To fellow BICC Trainsters:
Cherry Adair, Chris Pacheco, Eileen Wilks, Susan Plunkett,
Pam Johnson, Lynn Johnson, Ruth Schmidt, Karen Barrett,
Myrna Temte and Cheryl Harrington. Thanks, gals!
I couldn't have done it without you.

Books by Judith Bowen

HARLEQUIN SUPERROMANCE

689—THE MAN FROM BLUE RIVER
739—THE RANCHER'S RUNAWAY BRIDE*
791—LIKE FATHER, LIKE DAUGHTER*
814—O LITTLE TOWN OF GLORY
835—THE DOCTOR'S DAUGHTER*
872—HIS BROTHER'S BRIDE*
900—THE RANCHER TAKES A WIFE*
933—BORN IN A SMALL TOWN
"THE GLORY GIRL"
950—A HOME OF HIS OWN*
1020—ZOEY PHILLIPS**
1026—CHARLOTTE MOORE**
1032—LYDIA LANE**

HARLEQUIN SINGLE TITLE

WEST OF GLORY*

*Men of Glory
**Girlfriends

CHAPTER ONE

EVA HAINES hadn't been on the island a week before she realized she was being watched.

The feeling was unmistakable. Creepy. Eyes on her back, watching her from the forest on the other side of the creek as she scythed the knee-high grass near the house. Or from the wooded area behind the old, overgrown garden as she nailed plywood over broken windows. Or…from *somewhere.*

The first few days she hadn't paid much attention. She was too busy getting set up for the summer to worry about weird feelings and imaginings—too busy dusting, cleaning, ferrying over foodstuffs and supplies from Half Moon Bay in the aging fiberglass runabout with its tattered dodger and temperamental Mercury outboard. Besides, she was quite sure she was alone.

The weather had been fine, which had made her frequent trips to the mainland easier, and if there was one thing she'd learned from a childhood spent on or near the water under her sea dog father's demanding eye, it was how to fiddle with a temperamental outboard. Her unseen companion? Most likely an owl hidden in some monumental cedar tree keeping track of the intruder from the city. Or a vigilant nesting osprey. Or a rabbit. There were no bears on Liberty Island and Eva didn't believe in ghosts.

Eva was spending part of her summer vacation tidying up affairs for an eccentric distant relation, a cousin of her mother's, who'd broken her hip in the spring and who, at eighty-six, would not be returning to Liberty Island to live. *Be prepared.* Eva didn't want any surprises, so her first task had been to get everything shipshape for the two or three weeks she'd be occupying Doris Bonhomme's ramshackle house. That meant laying in plenty of oil and wicks for lamps, a spare propane tank for the kitchen range and refrigerator, among other necessities.

She wasn't bothering with gasoline for the emergency generator, which she didn't expect to have to use. What constituted an emergency on Liberty Island, where she and her sisters had spent the happiest summers of their childhood? Not being able to get *Jeopardy* on the ancient rabbit-eared black-and-white Motorola that Doris fired up occasionally to, as she put it, "keep in touch"? Definitely not!

But kerosene and candles were necessary. Jack Haines, who'd spent as much of his life as he could on or near the sea, had taught her well: only fools depend on luck.

Alone? Hey, what was she talking about—she had Andy to keep her company. She smiled, recalling how the ancient donkey had kicked up his heels, baring worn yellow teeth in a joyous hee-haw welcome when she'd first arrived. Then he'd bucked and galloped in an awkward circle just to show her how frisky he still was. Andy had been left to fend for himself when his mistress had been airlifted to the hospital and taken from there to a care home at the insistence of her doctor. Although Doris had reluctantly agreed that she could no longer look after herself in her isolated island home, she insisted that her beloved donkey was too old to uproot.

"I'm not putting that poor dumb creature through what I've been through," she told Eva, during a visit to Saint Mary's Hospital, shortly after Doris's accident. "He's too loyal. He doesn't deserve such a fate at his time in life. Your dad will know what to do."

And he had. Jack had arranged for a farmer from a nearby island to check on the animal, dumping off hay weekly, and treats like apples and carrots.

It wasn't as though either he or Doris would dream of requesting assistance from Doris's *actual* neighbor at the other end of Liberty Island. If, indeed, anyone still lived there…

It was so stupid, really. Eva's gaze strayed to the long thin crescent of land that stretched eastward, curving south, thick dark woods all the way to the rocky headland. The Bonhommes and the Lords hadn't spoken for fifty years, not since Doris had quarrelled with Hector Lord. What about? No one knew. There'd been a house once, nestled in the trees somewhere. Eva had never actually set foot on the Lords' side of the island. As a child, she hadn't dared; as a grown-up, now, she hadn't gotten around to exploring yet. Her mother, who'd been a girl at the time of the upset, had divulged various details—that the Lord house had been grand, that Hector had been a tall, dark, handsome man, wildly attractive to women, that the family had money, *pots* of money, as Eva recalled her mother's expression. Eva and her sisters had always imagined the Lords' money—*pots* of it—like pirate booty, gold and jewels spilling out of thick oaken sea chests and massive porcelain Chinese jars.

Doris herself had never spoken of the matter. As far as she was concerned, the island ended where her property did, at the creek, and plunged in a perfectly severed line, as though chopped with an ax, straight into the sea.

Hector Lord was long dead and Eva had no idea who owned that half of the island now. A trust? Heirs? The house had probably fallen into its cellar and grown over with ferns and moss. It wouldn't take many years to obscure all signs of any habitation in the fecund West Coast climate.

Certainly, there'd been no sign of life in the five days since she'd arrived: no smoke, no lights, no whine of outboards. Eva sighed and headed back to the *Edie B.* to retrieve the rest of the supplies she'd brought from the mainland that afternoon. How silly of Doris to nurse a grudge for so long. Fifty years!

Speaking of Andy—where was he? The donkey usually met her at the dock when she tied up after a trip to Half Moon Bay but he wasn't there now.

Eva's task this summer included finding a new home for the donkey. Most of the old woman's assortment of worldly goods would be discarded or go to thrift stores, but it was her dearest wish that her property become a marine park eventually, one of a chain that ran north and south through the Gulf Islands of the coast of British Columbia. The Bonhomme half could be signed over to a marine park trust—and that was something else Eva was investigating—but, of course, Doris had no control over the part she didn't own.

Finding a home for Andy would be a challenge. How long did donkeys live, anyway—forever? This one didn't look as though he'd suffered spending nearly three months on his own in the company of seals and seagulls and the elusive handful of wild goats that were supposed to live somewhere on the island—*that was it!*

Eva straightened and put her hands on her hips, blowing a stray lock of hair from her hot face. The half-empty runabout rocked gently, but she adjusted her stance so automatically she didn't even notice the motion. Why hadn't she thought of the *goats?* She gazed inland, past the woods, past the gentle rise where Doris's house stood, well back from the sea, to Abel's Peak, the rocky pinnacle that marked the high point on the island a good quarter mile behind the house. The water supply for the house originated up there, in an ancient stone-and-timber dam that funneled spring water to both Doris's house and, at one time, the residence on the other side of the island.

Of course! It was probably a goat she'd sensed when she'd been so certain someone—or something—was watching her. Like Jedadiah Island nearby, Liberty Island was rumored to be home to long-abandoned goat colonies, which some said went back to the days when the Spaniards cruised the area, Cortes and Valdez and Galiano, mapping the coast for Spain in the 1700s and accidentally losing some of their shipboard livestock in the process.

Eva bent down to heave a carton of tinned goods to the seat of the boat, then supported it against her hip. Balancing carefully, she stepped onto the dock and deposited the box beside the pile she'd already unloaded. No one knew if the story was true. Just as no one knew if the legendary goats were, less romantically, a few escapees from a farm on a neighboring island that had clambered ashore during an especially low tide sometime in the last several decades.

Whatever. Next task—moving everything up to the house. That was a job for the boxy wheelbarrow, equipped with two large bicycle wheels that Eva had found in the woodshed the day she arrived. Doris recycled everything. The homemade cart did an admirable job of transporting freight from the dock. It also handled a decent load of firewood.

Eva began to trundle toward the house. In late afternoon, the building looked dark and rather forlorn under the shadow of the tall cedars and the lofty arbutus trees to the west of the overgrown garden. There were shingles missing from the roof and any paint that had ever existed on the siding had worn off long ago. No need for repairs now, not unless the marine park people wanted to fix it up for a caretaker's residence, which was highly unlikely.

The crunch of her shoes on the weedy shale and broken rock seemed overloud in the warm not-quite-evening air. There wasn't a stir of wind. She wished now she'd brought Freddie. Her father had offered his dachshund—"for protection," he'd said with a wink.

She wasn't worried about protection; simple companionship was more like it. At least Freddie would bark if anything *real* was lurking about.

Why hadn't she remembered the goats earlier, for heaven's sake? Before she'd gotten herself all worked up over nothing?

THE VISITOR was disturbing. No, not disturbing, more like bothersome. Annoying. A presence on the island that set his teeth on edge when he remembered that not only had she arrived just after midmonth, which was already a week ago, but she seemed to be fixing up the house and settling in. A mere summer visit, he hoped. The briefer, the better.

Only why would anyone in his or her right mind be visiting Liberty Island? Or fixing up the house? The old woman had been airlifted off when he'd found her unconscious and obviously in very bad shape a dozen yards from her back door, her cart overturned and firewood scattered on the rain-soaked ground beside her. He'd stabilized her as well as he could and had called for medical help and, when he was certain it was on its way—he could hear the rotors of the air ambulance—he'd gone inside her house, where he'd found her cellular phone on the windowsill over the sink. He'd tucked it into her limp hand and left.

She'd hate to think she'd needed help, certainly not from him. This way, if she was dazed enough, she might assume she'd had the cell phone in her apron pocket, where she *should* have kept it at her age, and had actually called for assistance on her own before passing out. Foolish old woman.

That was before Easter. It didn't appear as though she was coming back, which was just fine by him. He didn't like company. At least, not company that wasn't there at his invitation. She was too old and ornery to be here, anyway—a constant worry. How many times had he sent Matthew out to spy on her, make sure she was okay? Had enough firewood? Had tied her boat up properly so it wouldn't wash away with a coming storm? How often had he told Fanny that, under no circumstances, was she to wander past the creek that separated the properties? Checking up on the old woman wouldn't have been such a nuisance; it was making sure he and Matthew weren't seen so they could both—he and his foolish neighbor—maintain the pretence that he *wasn't* keeping an eye on her that was wearing.

He didn't want to look out for her. He was glad she'd stayed away. She was well over eighty; she should've left long ago. He didn't go so far as to wish her dead, just nicely settled into some warm, comfortable nursing home somewhere on the mainland. He imagined her watching afternoon television, cheating at cards, griping about the food, all the while squirreling away crusts of bread and half-eaten apples in her lingerie drawer.

As far as he knew, she had few friends and no close relatives, certainly not young, beautiful ones like this visitor. His first glimpse of her was still seared onto his retinas. *At The Baths.* No, with any luck, the Bonhomme side of the island would go on the block in the next year or so and he'd be there, ready to scoop it up. He'd always felt that Liberty Island was his, anyway; it was only a matter of opportunity and cold, hard cash.

Now this visitor—this *intruder*—was on his mind. Was she the new owner? Already? Impossible!

All his life, he'd hunted beauty, wherever it could be found. In the last half dozen years, he created a kind of beauty in gems and precious metals for the select few who appreciated his skill and could pay his price. Chancing upon the visitor when he'd walked to the bathing pools three days ago had been a feeling he ranked among the handful of the most moving experiences he'd ever had. Watching Vivian dance. Seeing Fanny for the first time, a saucy two-year-old. A midwinter blue moon. The otherworldly fire in the center of an uncut ruby....

He'd gone to what they'd always called The

Baths, a series of three round hollows carved from the rock by the tides and the action of the sea over millions of years. One of them, the pool farthest from the open water, was where he'd bathed daily, summer and winter, ever since he'd returned almost three years ago. This time, walking along the stony path etched into the lichens, he'd heard a splash. The screech of a raven. A few notes of a song—*in a woman's voice.*

He'd paused, cinching his towel tighter around his waist. Then, when he realized that someone was on *his* island, swimming in *his* pools, he crept closer. The third pool, the deepest, a basin with stone walls four or five feet above the water even at high tide, was most dangerous. Even though Fanny swam like a fish and never went anywhere without his dog, Bruno, she was forbidden to go near The Baths. Crude steps, hacked out of the rock, led to the water and somebody—some stranger—had obviously found and used them.

Probably a sailor from a passing yacht that had moored in the little V-shaped bay just offshore. He didn't bother to check, instead strode directly toward the basin. This was posted private property, dammit, no trespassers allowed. Couldn't people read?

Then he stopped. *A mermaid.* Wearing nothing but seawater and sunshine. She lay on her back, her hair floating like kelp, hands languorous at her sides, feet moving gently. A raven high in an arbutus tree nearby squawked—it had spotted him.

She didn't understand what the raven was trying to tell her. As he watched, she stuck her tongue out and waved at the bird. She whistled, splashed with her other hand, then turned and kicked smoothly, gliding forward. Her buttocks were white in the sun, against the still, deep green of the water, her back lightly tanned. He could see the strap marks from a bathing suit.

So she was at least of this world.

He took a deep shaky breath and stepped back, unwilling to show himself. He had no idea then that she was staying at the old woman's house, that she was, in fact, a real intruder. All he knew was the stab of awareness. Innocence, sensuality, the sinews, shapes and planes of youth, strength, physical perfection. The artist in him was stunned.

God help him, he lingered in the trees like a voyeur until she left the water, climbed to the top of the basin and picked up a towel under the arbutus tree to dry herself. He couldn't—would never—deny the stirrings of his belly. That, too, was a kind of beauty. And it had been a very long time since he'd been with a woman. But, no, he simply craved more of the primal image before him.

Woman, without shame, alone in this primeval garden.

Then, when she'd laughed and flicked her towel at the raven, which flapped heavily through the trees with hideous cries, he'd slunk away. She hadn't wanted anyone to see her naked, not even the bird.

It made him feel unclean. So he'd canceled his own daily swim and left, depositing the image in the bank of his memory, an image he knew he would draw on one day....

And that was that. Just serendipity, pure and sweet.

Until two days later, when he discovered she was no passing yachtswoman. She'd actually moved into the Bonhomme house and appeared to have every intention of staying, judging by the number of trips she made to the mainland for provisions.

Which meant she'd become a problem.

CHAPTER TWO

WHERE WAS ANDY?

Eva released the handle of the pump that brought water into the house from the stone cistern and peered out the small square window over the cast-iron pantry sink. The donkey had to be okay. He'd been on his own for months and was hardly going to get into trouble a week after she arrived. She pumped again, filled a pitcher and put the water in the propane-fired refrigerator, along with the eggs, cheese, milk and two bottles of sauvignon blanc she'd bought at the Half Moon Bay Store.

Now, what for supper? Eva opened a tin of cream of mushroom soup and warmed it up on the ancient combination propane-wood range that stood prominently in Doris's big country kitchen. She was saving the limited supply of propane for the refrigerator, so had kindled a fire in the old range.

How about a grilled cheese sandwich to go with the soup? Why not? She'd had some variation on soup and sandwiches nearly every day so far. Then, just to make a dent in the silence, Eva switched on the transistor radio on top of the refrigerator and rocketed around from cupboard to counter to table, getting out a plate, a spoon, a bowl, half dancing, half walking, until she felt silly and stopped.

A person *could* go a little silly here. Had Doris gone a bit weird living by herself on Liberty Island? Of course, she wasn't alone all the time. As a younger woman, Doris had traveled for three or four months every year, usually in the winter. Then there were the many visitors she encouraged. Every summer, Eva's family had spent several weeks on the island. She remembered her father holding forth in the porch swing, admiring the view, a bottle of rum on the floor and a thick paperback turned over beside it. Or, if the tide was right and he felt like it, he'd be out in Doris's rowboat, fishing for sand dabs and rockfish.

Eva's mother, Felicity, gossiped with her older cousins and whoever else happened to be visiting, pulled weeds in Doris's garden, and, if they came in August, helped her pick blackberries and put up her garden produce.

Eva recalled helping her mother and Doris, or playing with her sisters in the treehouse behind the garden. Was it still there? When there were other cousins around, they'd played house and cowboys, pirates and princesses—

What in the world? Eva stopped at the window

over the sink, spoon forgotten in her hand, dripping soup onto the old linoleum floor.

There in the distance, halfway to where the ground began to rise to Abel's Peak, was a small child and Andy and—and some kind of enormous black dog!

Eva rushed to the door and flung it open. "Andy!"

She caught her breath, wishing she hadn't shouted, not wanting to frighten the child but…there was no one there. She blinked and rubbed her eyes with the back of her hand, like a cartoon character.

No child. No dog. Just the old donkey clip-clopping over the rocky ground as he trotted toward the house.

EVA WENT TO BED that night thoroughly rattled. The wind had come up in the evening and she could hear loose shingles banging on the roof. She hoped it wouldn't rain, and if it did, she hoped the leaks weren't near her bed. If necessary, she'd move to the other bedroom across the small landing at the top of the stairs.

Eva had always prided herself on being a calm, sensible woman. She had grown up the unflappable one in a chaotic family. Her father, a professor of literature at the University of British Columbia, spent every spare moment on whatever boat he happened to own at the time, ignoring his wife and drinking too much. Felicity Haines, a sad, gentle person, had died of an aneurysm when Eva was twelve, and Eva still missed her desperately. Kate, her oldest sister and very much her father's daughter, had sailed away on a tall ships adventure when she was eighteen, had settled in Africa and was doing something noble for world peace, Eva believed. She hadn't seen Kate for three years. Her other sister, Leona, had married a farmer and now raised ostriches, organic field peas and children—five of them, at last count—in Alberta.

Eva, the youngest by six years, had steered a steady course, graduating from high school with honors, working in a doctor's office for two years and then taking a degree in education. She'd just finished her first year as a substitute teacher in three different elementary schools in Burnaby. The two terms with grade one and two classes had convinced her she'd made the right career choice. She'd adored her little gap-toothed charges and was almost sorry when June was over. In the fall, she hoped to land a permanent job, preferably in the Lower Mainland or Vancouver Island and preferably teaching kindergarten, although it didn't much matter, and she'd sent résumés all over the province.

It would be nice, though, to settle somewhere near her father, who was alone and sometimes lonely, she thought, retired and living on his houseboat on the Fraser River. Now that Eva was an adult and entirely independent, she'd grown fond of Jack Haines, willing to forgive him the excesses that had alarmed her as a child.

At twenty-five and a trained teacher, Eva Louise Haines was definitely not the sort of person who imagined things. She did not see dogs and children and then, the next minute, not see them. There was nothing wrong with her eyes.

The child had been *there* most definitely. Red shorts, a dirty once-white T-shirt, no shoes. Dark hair, lots of it, a large black dog. Maybe strayed from a party of picnickers that had landed on the island that afternoon while she was away? She'd been surprised to see that Andy was with them, especially considering the presence of the dog....

She'd *seen* them. Obviously, the child and the dog had run away before she could open the door to call the donkey. They'd disappeared into the Lord forest on the other side of the creek, not into thin air. Campers, picnickers, boaters, whatever—someone besides her was on the island. That little boy or girl belonged to *someone*.

Eva finally dozed fitfully, wishing yet again that she'd brought Freddie. First someone—or something—watching her. Now children and dogs that were there one minute and gone the next.

IN THE MORNING, Eva took a brisk walk to the western end of the island. She often walked that route along the shore, looking for things the tide had yielded overnight. Sometimes there was an odd-shaped bit of driftwood or an old running shoe or a clock, washed up from who knows where. Once she'd found a coconut. It amused her to imagine how these things had ended up in the water. That coconut—had it arrived at Liberty Island after months adrift from Tahiti or had it rolled off a yacht deck from a grocery bag? Often, sadly, all she found was garbage—soft drink bottles and plastic bags, chunks of Styrofoam and torn fish net.

This morning, what she wanted to find was evidence of whoever had brought the child and dog. But there was nothing. No spent campfires on the beach, no tracks in the sand, no dinghy pulled up on the beach or launch anchored offshore. The visitors had most likely left the island before nightfall.

Somewhat relieved, Eva spent the rest of the morning in the small parlor, sorting through stacks of music books and sheets of looseleaf with snatches of songs penned on them. Doris had been an accomplished musician in her youth. According to Eva's mother, she was a fine pianist with a lovely voice, who'd had a brief career as a professional singer. Why had a woman as talented and beautiful and flamboyant, by all accounts, isolated herself on Liberty Island at thirty-six years of age, after her husband's death? Eva wished she'd paid a little more attention to her mother's stories.

By noon, Eva had filled only one box for the thrift store at Sechelt. She kept stopping to play one or another of Doris's little songs on the ancient Mason & Risch piano, which, from the sound of it and the sticking E and F keys, hadn't been looked after in years. By two o'clock, when she'd resolved to go for a swim, she'd filled three boxes to give away and another box of photos and personal items.

Funny how Jack Haines, who'd been so indifferent to his own wife while she was alive, was so solicitous of his wife's elderly cousin now. Guilt, maybe? Her father's lack of interest in his family had always hurt Eva. She was glad their relationship was steadier now. Of course, with Kate and Leona far away and their mother dead, who did Jack Haines have to neglect anymore? Just her. And, these days, he tended to lean on her instead. She didn't mind.

Dependable Eva.

Andy accompanied her to the water's edge. Normally, when the tide was out, as it was now, Eva would have gone to the pools on the other side of the island, a place mysteriously known as The Baths when she was a child. The pools were in a sort of no-man's-land between the Bonhomme and Lord properties. After the strange experience of yesterday, plus the feeling she'd had that she was being watched, Eva didn't want to walk through the tangle of dark woods between the house and The Baths.

Silly, she knew. As a result, she had to wade a considerable distance over rocks and barnacles before the water was deep enough to swim. Then she forgot all about Andy and his mysterious friends, putting in, first, her usual swim between the shore and Angler's Rock, a large outcrop that marked the entrance to Doris's little harbor even at high tide; then she spent a pleasant half hour climbing around, looking for the Coast Salish petroglyphs she remembered from long-ago outings. One day, before the summer was over, she intended to bring paper and charcoal and take rubbings of the figures, which were old, possibly ancient images pecked into the surface of the rock by Indians who'd inhabited the area.

Andy cropped the short grass just up from the beach as Eva swam in. She raked back her streaming hair as she emerged and, peering through the clear, green water to avoid stumbling, navigated carefully over the kelp stones and mussel-encrusted rock on the bottom of the small bay. There were very few sandy beaches in the Gulf Islands.

When she looked up, the visitors were back, regarding her from the top of a large boulder at the tide line, fifty feet from the old wharf. The little girl—or was it a boy?—had on blue shorts today and a red-and-white striped T-shirt. No shoes, as yesterday. The sudden appearance of the pair surprised Eva, but at the same time she felt huge relief.

So she wasn't losing her mind. And the child obviously had someone taking care of her, providing clean clothes. The family must be camped on the other side of the island....

"Hello!" Eva called and waved. There was no response. She veered toward the boulder, still stepping carefully. He—or was it a she—couldn't be more than four or five years old.

The big black dog bounded toward Eva then stopped stiff-legged and barked. It wasn't a friendly bark, either. Andy butted his head comically against her left hip, nibbling at her swimsuit, seeking the treats she usually had for him. For once, Eva wasn't amused.

"Hey!" she called again, waving her hand and smiling. "Don't worry, I won't hurt you."

The child raised one hand in a hesitant response to Eva's gesture and then slipped off the rock. Eva stumbled forward, cursing the pebbles that hurt her feet and slowed her progress. Where were they—behind the boulder? Across the creek? Into the woods on the other side?

If not, they'd vanished into thin air again!

Eva didn't know what to do. This was just too strange. Who *was* this little kid, out yesterday and today just—just wandering! Where was the mother? The father?

She needed to get dressed quickly and do some exploring. Find out, once and for all, where these people were camped and why no one was keeping an eye on this child.

EVA USUALLY RINSED OFF in the small, cramped bathroom off the kitchen, the only one in the house. Doris's bedroom had been downstairs, too, a more convenient arrangement for an elderly woman. Today, though, Eva just grabbed a towel from the bathroom cupboard and hurried up the stairs to her small bedroom under the eaves.

She stripped out of her bathing suit and toweled off, glancing out the small, paned window toward the sea. The rough, line-dried cotton almost hurt her skin. Andy had followed her and was grazing on the sparse grasses that grew between the house and the beach. No sign of the other two, though…

Eva's heart was racing. Ordinarily, she was a person who very much minded her own business. Live and let live, was her guiding principle. It had helped her survive a difficult family, demanding employers and several classes full of fractious six- and seven-year-olds.

Doris Bonhomme owned half of this island. As her agent, in effect, Eva had a duty to make sure that everything was all right, and that included checking up on any small visitors who might be lost or need her assistance.

Even if she *hadn't* been standing in for Doris, she would have wanted to get to the bottom of this.

Eva pulled on a pair of khaki shorts and a long-sleeved T-shirt and grabbed a tube of sunscreen from the top of the small antique dresser. She had sneakers by the kitchen door.

She paused before she left the room, catching a glimpse of herself in the spidery, ghosted mirror over the dresser—face hot, eyes bright, wet hair hanging in dark, thick ropes. She was actually going to the other side of the island....

The forbidden side.

Eva ran down the steeply pitched stairs in her bare feet.

"Hi."

The child—a little girl—was in her kitchen!

CHAPTER THREE

EVA WAS SO SURPRISED she didn't even notice that the sunscreen had slipped out of her hand and bounced down the last two steps onto the floor. The dog, who'd accompanied the girl into the house and parked himself at the door, growled menacingly.

"Oh, don't mind him. He's just my silly old dog. He's Bruno," the girl said airily, favoring Eva with a casual wave of her small hand. "He's 'bout as scary as a fruit fly, that's what Auntie Aggie says. Who're you? Are you the old lady? You're old but you don't look *that* old—"

"I-I'm Eva," Eva said, bending down to pick up the sunscreen. The dog, apparently a Newfoundland, now that she saw him up close, rumbled again and Eva gave him a hard look. He flopped onto the floor, stretched his massive black head over his paws and sighed. "What's your name?"

"Fanny. Do you live here?" Fanny gazed admiringly around the kitchen, although Eva couldn't see what there was to admire. "I thought somebody named Doris lived here. *She's* the old lady, I guess.

That's a nice mirror.'' She pointed to the spidery, cracked, unframed mirror over the dry sink. ''I always wanted to go in this house but I'm not allowed.'' She leaned toward Eva and covered her small mouth with her hand for a few seconds, then whispered loudly, ''I'm not sup-posed-ta be here so don't tell anybody, okay?'' She frowned at her dog, too, but the Newfoundland ignored them both.

''Would you like some lemonade?'' The girl and her dog were her first visitors.

''Got any pop?'' The girl looked hopeful. Her skin was a pale mocha, not from the sun. She was obviously of mixed racial heritage—Caucasian? Caribbean? Hawaiian?—fine-boned and fragile-looking, but judging from the way she talked, probably older than she seemed. Her eyes were big and honey-brown, her hair a riot of ringlets and curls. ''I *like* pop!''

''Sorry,'' Eva said, opening the refrigerator. ''Just lemonade.'' She reached for the pitcher, then realized the girl had moved deftly under her arm and was standing in front of her, gazing at the refrigerator's contents.

''Too bad,'' the child said, glancing up. ''I like lemonade, all right, but I *really* like pop and I'm not allowed to have any. It's nice in here! I like fridges. What's that? Is that wine? My dad likes wine.''

She pointed to a large green bottle of Perrier.

So does my dad, Eva thought. "No, it's water. Fizzy water. Do you want some with your lemonade?"

The girl considered, one finger on her lower lip. "Sure!" she said, brightly, then added, "I mean, yes, *please!*"

Eva poured two glasses, three-quarters lemonade, the rest Perrier, leaving the refrigerator door open. Who'd have dreamed the contents of an ordinary fridge could be so entertaining? Then she returned the bottle and pitcher to the fridge, shut the door and handed the child a glass.

"Cheers!" Fanny held up her drink, then laughed. It was a magical sound, sheer delight, and Eva couldn't help responding with a smile of her own. "Now we can be friends! *People* friends," the child added mysteriously. She sniffed at her drink cautiously and wrinkled her nose before taking a sip.

"To people friends." Eva clinked her glass gently against the child's. She supposed that was in contrast to *dog* friends. "Are you visiting the island with your family?"

"Oh, no. I live here." The girl gestured with one hand. "It's really *my* island. Mine and my dad's. You're the one who's the visitor, right, Bruno?" The dog opened one eye briefly and shut it again.

"You *live* here?" Eva stared. "Where?" If the child was staying on this island, if her parents were squatters or summer campers, that might account for the feeling Eva'd had of being watched for the past week. This child, who seemed to pop up out of nowhere, had probably been observing her from various hiding places. Or her parents or caregivers had. Eva felt a shiver trickle down her spine.

"Over there," Fanny said, waving vaguely in the direction of the creek. She marched to the cabinet beneath the mirror and wrenched open a drawer. "Boy, it's fun talking to you! Is that your lipstick?" She smiled and held up a tube, then pulled the top off. "Auntie Aggie has lipstick but she never puts it on unless she's going to the store or the doctor or something. Can I put some on?"

Before Eva could stop her, the girl had drawn a big red arc across her mouth. "That's not my lipstick, it belongs to the old lady who owns this house. But," Eva finished lamely, "I guess she wouldn't mind if you tried it out." The drawer still held an assortment of Doris's cosmetics, brooches and hairpins, most destined for the trash when Eva got around to cleaning it out. Anything of a personal nature that Doris wanted had already been taken to her new home at Seaview Lodge.

"Lift me up." Fanny held her arms out to Eva. "I want to see how I look."

Eva obliged, feeling the thin warmth, the litheness of the squirming child in her arms as she held her up to the mirror. A small brown face gazed back at them both, the small, pursed mouth ribaldly framed in what Eva had always thought of as an old lady color—not orange, not red, not coral. Something useful that ''went'' with everything.

''Oh! It's funny!'' Fanny laughed and drew the back of her hand across her lips, smearing the lipstick. Eva laughed and briefly hugged her tight before putting her down.

Whoever this child was, wherever she'd come from, Eva was utterly charmed.

''I suppose you've got jewels and beads and earrings and all kinds of pretty things. Maybe you could let me play with them some—hey, is this your piano?'' Fanny had headed into the small parlor. ''We have a piano. Dad's teaching me to play.'' She sat on the wobbly stool and plunked out ''Old Macdonald Had a Farm.'' Eva clapped and the girl's eyes shone.

''Let's go into your yard now,'' Fanny suggested. ''We could have a picnic for the birds with stuff out of your fridge.''

''Hold on.'' Eva decided it was time to get some answers. Someone would—*should*—be looking for Fanny soon. ''Do you live with your mom and dad?''

''Just my dad,'' the girl said, shooting a look Eva's way as she examined the covers on several magazines piled on the sofa. ‘‘And Auntie Aggie and Uncle Matthew and Bruno and the squirrels and George the big black bird that lives in our tree and—’’

‘‘Are you camping? Do you live in a tent or a boat?’’

‘‘A boat?’’ She giggled. ‘‘We have a big house and I have my own room and a playhouse in a tree and everything.’’ Fanny frowned at Eva as though she was particularly dense. ‘‘I told you, this is *my* island. Mine and my dad’s.’’

‘‘But where *is* everyone? Who’s looking after you now?’’

‘‘Bruno.’’ Fanny was obviously surprised by the question. ‘‘I’m not supposed to go anywhere without Bruno. He’s my good old dog, aren’t you, Bruny?’’ The Newfoundland had accompanied her to the parlor; he glanced adoringly at the girl as she patted his broad head. ‘‘And Auntie Aggie looks after me, too. She looked after my dad when he was little. And sometimes Uncle Matthew and my dad look after me, too, but my dad works a lot and I’m not supposed to ’sturb him—’’

The sudden sound of a mechanical doorbell clanging, a horrible rusted sound that blended with a loud series of barks from Bruno, made Eva jump. Doorbell? She didn’t even know there *was* one.

‘‘Yikes!’’ The child’s eyes were huge. ‘‘I bet

that's Uncle Matthew.'' She tore through the French doors that stood open to the back garden. Her dog bounded after her.

''Anybody here?'' An angry male voice preceded another insistent buzz, followed by the hammering of fists on the door. ''Open up!''

Fanny—

Eva ran to the door, putting her hand on the knob just as it burst open.

''You see a little girl around here?'' A man stood in the doorway. His eyes, blue-green as the sea, blazed into hers.

''Yes! I mean—no!'' Eva swallowed. She hadn't heard the entire story from Fanny yet. She didn't have a good feeling about any of this. If this was the uncle who was in charge, why did he allow the child to wander—

''Which is it?'' His eyes darted around the kitchen and he took a step forward. Eva grabbed his arm and he stared down at her. ''Yes or no?''

''I haven't invited you in, *sir,*'' she managed to say through clenched teeth. His arm was rock hard. He was tall and strong and looked to be in his mid-thirties, handsome in a careless way, with several days' growth on his face and unruly sunbleached brown hair. ''I don't believe we've met.''

He shook off her hand. ''Where's Fanny?''

''She's not here,'' Eva burst out, truthfully, adding, not so truthfully, "I don't know what you're talking about!"

Then she yelped as he pushed past her and strode into the parlor. Outraged, Eva was right on his heels, relieved to glance out into the sunny overgrown garden behind the house and see neither girl nor dog.

"I swear I heard the damn dog bark," the man muttered, almost to himself. He stepped to the open French doors. *"Fanny! Where are you?"*

Eva held her breath. There was no answer. She didn't think there would be.

Without a backward glance, the man stepped into the yard and purposefully set off toward the tumbledown fence that surrounded the yard and garden, Doris's pitiful attempt to keep out rabbits and other marauders. "Fanny!" He vaulted the fence and continued toward the creek.

Eva was torn. On the one hand, if this was Fanny's Uncle Matthew, everything *must* be okay. He was just searching for the child, who had obviously strayed without telling anyone where she was going. Eva couldn't blame him for being a little angry.

On the other hand, she didn't like his attitude, charging into her house the way he had....

Making up her mind, she ran after him. He had several minutes' head start and she saw him break into a lope thirty yards beyond the fence and veer toward one of the shallower creek crossings. He was fit and he clearly knew where he was going. And he had shoes on.

Eva didn't. Ouch! She stumbled on a rocky patch of ground, wishing she'd taken the time to retrieve her sneakers, which were still standing by the kitchen door. Too late now. If she didn't hurry she'd lose him—she'd lose them both—and, just in case the little girl needed her, Eva wanted to be on the scene when the man caught up.

If he did.

Secretly, Eva was rooting one hundred per cent for Fanny and the Newfoundland dog….

BY THE TIME Eva crossed the creek, stepping from rocks at the Bonhomme side, onto a slippery half-buried log festooned with algae, then onto several water-polished stones on the Lord side, Fanny's uncle had disappeared into the woods. She hurried along a faintly visible path etched into the stony soil.

"Excuse me?" she called, realizing how hopelessly ineffective her query was. "Yoo-hoo! Hello?"

All she heard back, faintly, was the sound of the man's voice calling the girl's name again, then whistling, presumably for the dog.

Eva was hot and her feet hurt. Why hadn't she

just stayed home? She heard a crash behind her—*My God!*

She wheeled. Andy appeared at the end of the path behind her, bobbing his head and breaking into a trot as he spotted her. Oh, for goodness sake. Eva's heart was pounding.

The uncle was chasing Fanny and the dog, she was chasing the uncle and now Doris's donkey was chasing her!

She let Andy catch up. He nuzzled the pocket of her shorts and she scratched his soft whiskery nose. "No snacks today, Mr. Andy."

This was ridiculous. She'd turn around and go back to the house and change into some jeans, a long-sleeved shirt, grab a hat, put on some socks and proper shoes. Then she'd thoroughly search the Lord half of the island. She wouldn't be able to sleep another night on this island not knowing what was going on with the little girl.

Okay. That was a plan. Accompanied by the donkey, Eva began to limp toward the creek again. She'd stepped on a thorn, probably from a rosebush or a blackberry thicket somewhere, blown onto the path. She leaned against a tree and inspected her heel, balancing on one leg. Her foot was so dirty she couldn't see where the thorn had gone in her foot.

"Hey!"

She turned. The man who'd burst into her kitchen was standing at the bend in the path she'd abandoned. Eva straightened and faced him. "Did you find her?"

"No." He shrugged, apparently not that worried. "She's probably home already."

"Home?"

"She knows these woods better than I do," he said, ignoring her question. He gave her a cursory glance, from her toes to still-damp hair hanging in ropes. "Something wrong with your foot?"

"Nothing serious," she said, instinctively rubbing her heel against her leg. "Just a rose briar. I'll be fine."

He surveyed her again, his eyes icy. "Shouldn't run around the woods without shoes on."

"I didn't know I'd be leaving so quickly!" She felt a trickle of perspiration inch toward her nose and wiped it with the back of her hand. "What do you mean by bursting into my house like that?"

"I thought Fanny might've gone in there alone, to play. You weren't answering the door—"

"I would have! If you'd had the courtesy to give me a few seconds!"

He shrugged again. "Sorry. Look, can I accompany you back to the house?"

"I'll be fine. I think you should take better care of that child. Today isn't the first time I've seen her.

She can't be more than five or six. What kind of uncle are you, letting her run around by herself like that? She could get lost or hurt...."

"Uncle?" He frowned. "What the hell are you talking about?"

"Aren't you her uncle Matthew?"

"Uncle Matthew?" He grimaced, an attempt at a smile. "Hell, no! I'm her father."

CHAPTER FOUR

THUMP!

Agnes Klassen winced as she smacked the lump of pastry with the side of her rolling pin. She didn't usually treat pie dough like this. "So what's your daddy going to say when he hears all *that?*"

The child's eyes were big and brown. "You going to tell him, Auntie Aggie?"

The housekeeper's glance slid sideways. "You think I should?" She wasn't sure what to make of Fanny's news. The girl had spent the past half hour chattering about her new friend at the other end of the island, the woman Aggie's husband, Matthew, caretaker of the Lord estate, had mentioned shortly after her arrival ten days ago. Matthew had said the visitor was harmless, just someone using the old woman's house for a holiday, and Aggie believed him.

Fanny was thrilled about the lipstick she'd tried, the magazines she'd looked at, even the contents of the visitor's fridge. Poor child! All alone and no playmates her own age. Was it any wonder she was starved for anything new?

Fanny said Silas had come looking for her, but she'd run through the visitor's back door and away through the forest, managing to get home first. The incident hadn't been mentioned at dinner the previous evening. Silas, of course, could be extremely absentminded. He had plenty to think about. Besides, he didn't tell his housekeeper everything, did he?

"I guess so," the child responded slowly, sticking her thumbs into the pastry Agnes had given her. "'Less I tell him first," she added quickly, then nodded, as though pleased with her decision. "How 'bout that? Maybe I better, since he was chasing me 'n' Bruno most of the way home. It was fun!"

With renewed enthusiasm, she began pressing her pastry into the five-inch tart pan Aggie reserved for Fanny's pies. "I know!" Her face was bright. "I'll tell him at the party today."

Aggie rolled out one quarter of the dough in front of her. She was making two pies this morning, one for their evening meal and one for the freezer. Both Silas and Matthew were inordinately fond of blueberry pie. What man wasn't? Aggie smiled at Fanny. You couldn't stay mad at the little rascal, she thought. No, you couldn't. Fanny had her—and

Matthew and Silas—twisted around her pinkie finger, always had.

Fanny's pie was for the party she was having that afternoon, presumably for her father and Bruno and the squirrel Aggie had never seen but knew all about—even that it went by the name of Kelly. A dog and a squirrel! Fanny needed more people in her life, the dear motherless waif.

Also on the menu were raw vegetables and cheese dip, Aggie's suggestion, and toast and cake and soft drinks, Fanny's request. Silas didn't believe in feeding children a lot of sugar, so that would mean carrot cake and cream cheese icing and juice boxes, not pop. Sometimes Aggie wondered where a man like Silas, who'd surely never expected to be a father, got so many definite notions about childrearing.

Actually, now that she thought about it, Aggie was *glad* Fanny had met the young woman staying in Doris Bonhomme's old house, although she disapproved of the way it had come about. She didn't like Fanny and that dog of hers skulking about the island, spying on folks. A five-year-old, no matter how clever for her age, should not be roaming around freely, talking to birds and chipmunks, hair uncombed, not even properly dressed half the time.

But you couldn't argue with Silas Lord! A more stubborn man had never lived. Aggie ought to know; she'd helped raise him herself, as housekeeper to

Silas's parents many years ago. Of course, in those days, she'd been constantly busy, cooking and cleaning for the Lord household both on Liberty Island and at their home in West Vancouver, as well as raising Ivor, their own boy. Matthew had done the outdoor work, still did although he was pushing seventy now.

They both were. She was sixty-eight and feeling every minute of it some days. She sighed and wiped one cheek with a floury wrist, aware of the aches that had crept up over the past few years. Silas was thirty-two, just a little younger than their Ivor, all grown-up, too, and in an assisted-living home in Gibsons, making his way, such as it was, in the world....

As a boy, young Silas had been as cheeky and charming as his small daughter was today.

"What's a good time for my party, Auntie?" Fanny stared at the wall clock, pretending to read it, a pencil crayon in one hand and a piece of paper in front of her on the table.

"How about two o'clock?" Aggie suggested. "That way you won't spoil your supper."

"The big hand is on the twelve for an 'o'clock,' right?" Fanny took a fresh pencil crayon, orange, and drew a large circle on the piece of paper in front of her. The child didn't really know how to tell time, but she understood about the big hand and the small hand. Aggie had watched Silas coach her patiently, right there at the big wooden table in the kitchen, going through the A-B-C's, teaching her to tell time, name the days of the week, tie her own shoes. He'd started music lessons recently on the old out-of-tune player piano in the parlor—Aggie had often heard her plunking out "Old Macdonald" after breakfast—and he'd taught her to swim and play croquet.

"And the little hand is on the?" The housekeeper waited, floury hands held high as she crossed to the sink.

"Two!" Fanny triumphantly held up two fingers, then added a 2 to her drawing, not exactly in the right spot, but close enough.

"And what is that you're drawing, honey?"

"It's a 'vitation," Fanny said earnestly. "You know—that you send out? This gives when. I'm going to draw my little gypsy house for the place. When you have a party, you have to send 'vitations, don't you?"

"Well, of course you do," Aggie agreed, rinsing her hands in a basin in the sink. She wondered where a squirrel got mail. Fanny's "little gypsy house" was the caravan playhouse Silas had built for her under the trees in the old orchard. The girl wanted for nothing money could buy. "Anything else you'll need?"

"Some wool," the girl returned promptly. "I

need a ball of that nice yellow wool you're knitting me a sweater with. Can I have some?''

''For decorations?'' Aggie reached for a kitchen towel, mystified, doubly so as she observed Fanny's sudden self-conscious, rather evasive expression.

''Well...'' The girl nibbled on the end of the pencil crayon for a few minutes, examining her drawing. Then she looked up, dark eyes dancing. ''*Something* like that!''

EVA SLEPT amazingly well, considering the events of the previous afternoon, and it was nearly ten when she awoke to the sound of shingles banging on the roof again.

After breakfast, she dragged the cumbersome wooden ladder from the shed to the house and climbed up to drive in a few nails. There was a musty stack of shingles in the shed, of various patterns, as well as other odds and ends. Pieces of lumber, screws and nails in jam tins, wire screening, rusted tools of various kinds. Eva wondered if Doris had done all her own repairs. She was coming to a new appreciation of what it took to live here all alone, as Doris had for so long.

At least the riddle of the child and dog was solved, and Eva could focus on the task ahead of her, tidying up Doris's affairs. Fanny obviously lived with her father, Silas Lord, at the other end of the island. Simple. There *were* Lords using the old family place. She should've been told. Why hadn't Doris said anything?

''Uncle'' Matthew, Eva'd been informed, was the caretaker; ''Auntie'' Aggie was his wife, the housekeeper. Fanny's father hadn't offered much more than that before he'd turned abruptly, at her repeated refusal of his help, and headed back down the path.

She'd hobbled home and managed to dig the briar out but her heel was still sore. What a strange man. What a strange child! Eva still wasn't sure she believed Fanny and her family were actually living on Liberty Island year-round. A summer could seem like a very long time to a young child. Spending the summer here alone, probably bored, could account for Fanny's interest in Doris's house. Of course, little girls were interested in lipstick and jewelry and dress-up, but the contents of fridges? Old broken mirrors? Magazine covers?

She'd been more than inquisitive, positively nosy. In a way, Eva admired her brashness. *Ask and ye shall receive....* A contrast to what Eva remembered of her own childhood. She'd been on the shy side, polite and accommodating—too polite, Doris had always said, teasing both her and her mother, Felicity, so inaptly named, a woman who'd had more than her share of unhappiness in her short life.

Eva finished sorting through the sheet music and

other musical paraphernalia in the so-called music room, a glass-enclosed room that looked to the sea on the south and had French doors leading to the patio on the north. Instead of a swim, she decided to go for a run along the beach. She'd be ready for a late lunch when she returned.

Eva ran in shorts, a tank top and sneakers. The pebbly beach, interspersed with grassy areas and patches of sand, was too rough to run in bare feet, even if she hadn't had a sore heel. The breeze was welcome, light against her overheated face, and as she approached the house on her way back, she slowed to a brisk walk, reaching up to whip off the scarf that held back her hair.

Whew! Looked like another summer scorcher of a day. A shower, a sandwich and then—

What was that? A square of colored paper lay just inside the door of the house. The door was always unlocked; Eva wasn't even sure there was a lock. What was there to keep out? Just Andy and the rabbits that nibbled Doris's garden…

Eva stooped to pick up the envelope, and smiled as she turned it over. It was clearly handmade, a little crooked and dripping with glue. From Fanny. Eva opened it and a small loop of yellow wool fell out.

She bent to retrieve it. Inside the envelope was a

much creased piece of paper, which Eva unfolded, her smile widening.

There were no words. Just a drawing of a playhouse of some sort, with a table and chairs outside and various kinds of food on the table—a huge cake, drinks with straws. Nothing was in proportion; it was a typical four- or five-year-old's drawing. A clock face, drawn in orange, showed two o'clock. It was just past one now. There was a patch of glue with telltale yellow wisps caught up in it next to the rendition of a clock face. Eva glanced at the yellow loop on her wrist, the yarn that had fallen out of the envelope. Aha!

Then she turned to gaze toward the creek that separated the Bonhommes' from the Lords'. A yellow loop waved gently in the breeze, suspended from a bush on the far side of the creek.

While she'd been gone, *someone* had been very busy....

CHAPTER FIVE

SILAS HAD A STUDIO set in the trees well away from the house in a building that had once been reserved for staff. The Klassens lived with him and Fanny in the main house, a large shingle-sided two-and-a-half-story dwelling, built in a rather grand post-Victorian style nearly one hundred years before by his great-grandfather. The Lords and the Bonhommes, who'd settled at the other end of the island, had been business partners once, lumber barons cutting virgin timber on Vancouver Island at the turn of the century, a time when many family fortunes had been made in British Columbia.

Because there was no electricity on the island and because the studio was some distance from the house, which had a generator for essential electrical needs, Silas created jewelry as it had been created for thousands of years, using hand tools to work the precious metals and a propane-fired forge. At present, he was working on a commission from a Toronto auto parts mogul, a gift for his wife's fortieth birthday. Six months earlier, Silas had delivered a magnificent diamond-and-opal bracelet to the same man—for his mistress's birthday.

The current project incorporated tanzanite, a gemstone Silas particularly liked, set into the silver-and-gold neckpiece, bracelet and earrings. Without artificial light, daytime hours were precious and Fanny knew she could only interrupt him in his studio if it was important. This morning when he'd come back from The Baths—no sign of the visitor today—he'd found one of Fanny's handmade envelopes in the willow basket outside his open studio door.

Silas shook his head. Parties! Was his daughter turning into a social animal like her mother? Fanny seemed to generate an excuse to have a party every couple of days.

Not that he minded. And he always humored her. Silas never forgot that he was the one who'd brought his daughter into these isolated circumstances on Liberty Island nearly three years ago and he'd do anything in his power to make sure she was happy here. Summer was a fine time, when Fanny could be a free spirit, safely wandering the forest and the shore with her dog. Winters were much harder.

Today's event was most likely because of what had happened yesterday. Fanny hadn't mentioned the incident at dinner—and neither had he—but he suspected the party was by way of an apology. She knew the old woman's house was forbidden, whether vacant or occupied. Indeed, that entire end of the island was off-limits; she wasn't even to cross the creek.

But he could understand that she'd been tempted. The newcomer must have been too much to resist. He didn't blame Fanny. No other children around. No guests. Silas had no appetite for society, and it had been many months since he'd invited anyone to Liberty Island, other than the Klassens' son, Ivor. His occasional trips to his studio in Vancouver fulfilled any needs he might've had for company, male or female. Nor had he intended to meet the island's visitor, never mind under such odd circumstances. Busting into her kitchen and tearing through her house, no less! He was a little embarrassed about that.

Hell, he'd been scared. He'd looked everywhere for Fanny, in all her usual places, but she hadn't been in any of them. Not in her tree house at the bottom of the garden. Not in her playhouse he'd built for her in the old orchard. Or in her room, playing with dolls, or up in the attic, where she'd found trunks of old clothes that had belonged to Silas's grandmother and often played dress-up, sometimes draping even Bruno with a hat or scarf.

Silas had hoped the visitor would simply leave and that would be that. He admitted to some curiosity—why hadn't she come wandering to the eastern side of the island before this? Why had she kept—as far as he could tell—so carefully to the Bonhomme property, except for that excursion to The Baths? He'd only seen her there once and the bathing pools, admittedly, had always been a sort of neutral territory. Still, how could she know that?

Silas glanced at the old-fashioned Rolex he wore. He'd freed himself from many of his big-city habits, including locking doors, which made no sense on Liberty Island, but he'd never been comfortable without the Rolex, which he'd worn ever since his grandfather, Hector Lord, had given it to him a few months before the old man had died.

Silas didn't miss much of his previous life. The days of catching an afternoon flight to Paris for the weekend, or disappearing to Mexico at a moment's notice to share a workbench with the silver masters in Taxco for a few months, or flying to Amsterdam twice a year to buy the rough diamonds he used in his work, then whisking off to Singapore to have them faceted and ground. Now that he'd begun living on Liberty Island again, he didn't miss the once essential Palm Pilot, but the Rolex, one of the few personal mementos he had of a scattered family, stayed on his wrist.

Silas remembered clearly the day the old man had given it to him. He'd arrived home from university to announce he'd dropped out of business school and was going to Milan to study art. His parents had been furious—as Silas had expected—but the old man had beckoned him into a back room, where he'd taken off the watch and handed it to him with a chuckle. "Here, my boy. It belongs to you." No further explanations.

Hector Lord had been dead for nearly fourteen years.

Almost two o'clock…

Idly, Silas wound the watch as he strode toward the orchard. When Fanny had begun staging her little events earlier that summer, he'd sometimes offered to help carry her supplies to wherever she was holding the party. Her playhouse. The promontory where they had picnics. Or, most difficult for him, her tree house behind his studio. He couldn't climb up there as easily as he'd done when the tree house had belonged to him and Ivor. Fanny was always deeply offended at his suggestion, as only Fanny could be, insisting she could—and would—do everything herself. She was independent, all right. Sociable and sassy. Loving.

She was everything in the world to him, the center of his life.

When he arrived, five minutes early, she was setting out cups and plates on a table in front of the playhouse, which he'd designed and then had built and painted, with Matthew's help, to resemble a miniature gypsy caravan. Everything was built on a three-fifths scale, perfect for a child.

"Hi, Dad!" Fanny had a temper but she couldn't hold a grudge for very long. It was another of her characteristics he adored. She certainly didn't get it from his side of the family. No matter what had come between them—and they had plenty of disagreements—her sunny spirits would bubble over and she'd forget her outrage in a minute.

"What's the occasion?" He took one of the solid and squarely built little wooden chairs ranged around the small blue-painted table and sat down. "Kelly's birthday?"

She gave him an arch look and continued setting out cups and plates, places for six, he observed. "It's a surprise, Daddy. I can't tell you," she said, then continued a little worriedly, "I don't know when Kelly was actually borned so I don't know when to have a party for him."

Silas's personal theory was that the little gray squirrel Fanny was so fond of was already a generation or two past the original "Kelly." How long did squirrels live? "*Born,* honey, not *borned,*" he automatically corrected.

"*Born,*" she repeated under her breath, counting out the cutlery. Silas watched as she went to the nearby doll carriage and pulled out a Tupperware container. "You can take the lid off this, please."

Silas pried the top off. "Mmm, cake."

Fanny nodded, looking pleased. "With icing. Auntie Aggie made it. What time is it now, Daddy?"

Silas checked his watch. "Five past two."

"No, 'xactly. What time is it 'xactly?"

"Okay." He studied his watch again. "It's six and a half minutes past two."

Fanny nodded, her face sober. She sighed, then put the cake in the middle of the table and went back to the doll carriage and pulled out more Tupperware containers. Vegetable strips. Some kind of nutritious-looking dip—trust Aggie. What would he have done these past few years without her and Matthew? Juice boxes. A plastic jug of water alive with ice cubes—

"*Now* what time is it, Daddy?"

"Ten past. Shall we get started?" Silas glanced at the five other places set at the table. "Is Auntie Aggie coming?"

"No. She said she's too busy. This one's for Bruno—" Fanny touched one plate, part of an unbreakable set she kept in the caravan. "And this one's for Kelly, 'cept I'm not sure he's coming." Silas hadn't heard the squirrel. Kelly rarely "visited" but, when he did, he made his presence known by his loud chirruping from the huge Orenco apple tree behind the playhouse.

''Matthew's gone over to Half Moon Bay, if you're expecting him,'' Silas told her. ''He won't be back until just before dinner.''

''No.'' She shook her head. ''Auntie Aggie told me that already so I didn't make him a 'vitation. What time is it now—*hey!*''

There was a distinct clip-clop on the packed earth of the path that led toward the wharf. The donkey! Of course.

Silas turned to see the grizzled old beast clatter into view, head bobbing. He'd been a fixture on their side of the island, off and on, for months. Harmless enough, from what Silas had seen. Probably lonely, too, although Silas knew someone had made arrangements for weekly hay drop-offs in the spring. Bruno sat up, ears perked, eyes interested.

This was the ''surprise''?

''Andy!'' Fanny cried out. The animal had a name? How did Fanny know— ''—and *Eva!*''

''Am I late?'' The woman who'd moved into the Bonhomme house stepped from the wooded path into the clearing. She was dressed in jean shorts and a pink T-shirt and had her dark hair tied back in a ponytail. Her left arm, oddly, was festooned with what seemed to be loops of yellow yarn. *Eva.* Silas stood automatically, as he'd been taught to do when a member of the opposite sex entered the room—he supposed this arrangement under the apple tree qualified as a room.

Fanny clapped her hands in delight. "Surprise!" she crowed. "Surprise! Surprise!" Silas heard the squirrel start to chatter in the tree overhead. So Kelly had joined them, after all....

The afternoon, which had promised to be just another hot, somewhat boring July afternoon, had suddenly become interesting.

EVA'S FIRST THOUGHT—that Fanny's father might have had something to do with the party invitation—evaporated when she saw his expression, as dismayed, she was sure, as her own. He hid his surprise instantly and stepped forward, hand extended. "We weren't properly introduced yesterday. Maybe we should start again. I'm Silas Lord." He nodded. "Welcome."

"Eva Haines." She shook his hand briefly, aware of the heat of his skin, the hard, dry strength of his fingers....

At his reference to their previous encounter, the way he'd practically thrown her to the side as she grabbed his arm to prevent him from barging into her kitchen, her lips thinned, and she answered him coolly. "I'm sorry I'm late."

"You're limping," he said bluntly, leading her toward the small table.

"Yes." She didn't elaborate. The briar she'd removed must have left something behind, because her heel had begun to throb that morning. She'd stuck on a Band-Aid after her run and had worn thick socks with her sneakers.

"It's a party!" Fanny, at least, was delighted to see her. "This is my dad, I guess you know that—" Silas nodded again "—and this is my playhouse he builded for me and this is Bruno, well, you know *him!*" She waved toward the branches overhead. "And that's Kelly up there, he's my squirrel."

Eva dutifully peered up but didn't spot the source of the scolding. She waved and called softly, "Hi, Kelly!" then felt rather silly, knowing Silas Lord was watching. Her initial impulse had been to enter into the child's game, her play "world," just as she'd have done with one of her students at school.

When she turned, Fanny's father was indeed watching her.

He gestured toward a small chair opposite his, and Eva approached. "Are you in the habit of talking to squirrels? And what, if I might enquire, is that unusual bracelet you're wearing? It's very attractive. Did my daughter make it for you?"

"Dad!" Fanny giggled.

Eva lifted the loops from her wrist and set them on the table. "You could say that. I found my way here by following the yarn Fanny left on the bushes. That was very clever of her.''

Fanny beamed. ''I wanted you to draw me a map, Dad, but then it wouldn't be a surprise.''

Silas met Eva's eyes. ''I'm guessing you got an invitation, just as I did.''

''Yes.''

''And you followed the clues. Kind of like Hansel and Gretel.''

Eva laughed. ''Exactly. Except the birds didn't eat up all the clues, like they ate the crumbs—''

''I know that story!'' Fanny interrupted, coming to the table and looking important as she picked ice cubes out of the beverage container with her fingers and put one in each of the three plastic glasses in front of her. ''Dad reads that story to me.''

''No birds to eat up all the crumbs,'' Silas said in a low voice, his eyes on Eva's, ''and no big bad witch at the end of the trail, either.''

Eva hesitated for a split second, then shook her head. ''No.'' Fanny's father seemed very different today from the man she'd met yesterday. Then he'd been brusque and determined, angry and arrogant, with the exception of those few minutes on the trail when he'd returned, almost as an afterthought, to offer to escort her back to Doris's house. Was that to make sure she left the property? This afternoon he seemed deliberately friendly, even jovial.

"Except Auntie Aggie, of course," he teased, with a glance at his daughter. The half smile transformed his face, changing it from grim and rather formidable to handsome, even boyish. Which was the real Silas Lord?

"Dad!" Fanny shouted. "Don't say that! Auntie Aggie's not a big, bad witch. Here, have some." She pushed a glass toward her father.

Silas took a sip. "Mmm," he said, with a smile at his daughter over the rim. "Champagne! I suppose that's in honor of our visitor."

"It's not champagne, Dad," Fanny said seriously. "It's fizzy water and lemonade, just like I had at Eva's."

"Aha!" Silas put his glass down firmly. "So you *were* in the house, you little rascal!"

CHAPTER SIX

"YEP!" Fanny laughed. "Eva gave me a drink, only she didn't have any pop in her fridge, just like us. And me 'n' Bruno ran out of there when we heard you coming. *Ha!*"

Fanny gave her father a triumphant look. "And we beated you home, Dad!"

"*Beat,* honey," Silas corrected, his eyes locked on Eva's astonished gaze. "Not *beated.* And I think you should call our guest Miss Haines, don't you, Fanny? It *is* Miss, I presume," he continued smoothly.

"I'm not married," Eva blurted out, about to take a sip of the lemonade. She was astonished at the rapid interchange between father and daughter, then the sudden switch to her. She was beginning to feel like Alice at the Mad Hatter's picnic. "*Miss* is rather old-fashioned, isn't it? And, of course, Fanny, I want you to call me Eva. It's my name."

"And what does *Ms.* Haines do when she's not visiting Liberty Island?"

"I'm a teacher." Why was she answering this man's nosy questions so willingly?

"A teacher?" Fanny's father sounded genuinely interested. He studied her across the blue table and reached for his glass again. Fanny was busy serving pieces of cake on small plates. "High school?"

"No, elementary. I had grade one and two classes last year."

"Substitute?"

"Yes. I'm applying for several full-time positions for this fall, though."

"How is it you've come to Liberty Island? Are you related to Doris Bonhomme?"

Eva stared at him, her lips pressed firmly together. She felt her cheeks warm under his steady gaze.

"I wish *I* could go to school," Fanny said sadly. She licked icing from her fingers.

"Oh, you'll be in school soon enough," Eva said, glad to change the subject. "How old are you, Fanny?"

"Five-goin'-on-six," she responded, holding up one hand, fingers spread. That had been Eva's estimate, although the child was small for her age.

"You've just turned five, Fanny," her father said quietly and his daughter frowned. "That's hardly almost six."

"Well, I suppose you're going into kindergarten, then," Eva said hastily, aware that the subject of school seemed to have cast a pall on their little party for some reason.

"Nope." Fanny shook her head and sighed. "Kids in books go to school." Eva thought that was a strange comment but Silas immediately stood up and stepped away from the table.

"Would you like to see Fanny's playhouse? We can eat our cake and vegetables later. You'll have to bend over, I'm afraid, as it's not designed for grown-ups."

The awkward conversation was successfully derailed and Eva followed Fanny to the Dutch doors of the playhouse, which looked very gypsyish, even to the point of having wooden wheels, nonfunctional, she assumed. Silas didn't accompany them, which was a good thing, Eva realized, once she was inside. The small structure consisted of one rectangular room with two small upholstered chairs, a brick-look plywood false fireplace complete with painted flames and braided hearth rug, miniature rose-sprigged curtain-hung cupboards and a child-size bed, covered with a quilt and tucked into a nook in the wall. There was even a tiny wrought-iron shelf above the bed, with half a dozen books. Bent over as she was, Eva managed a quick glance at the titles: several worn Curious George stories, *Goodnight, Moon,* two tiny Beatrix Potter volumes, including Eva's personal favorite, *The Tale of Two Bad Mice,* and a well-thumbed older edition of Mother Goose nursery rhymes.

This place was a child's dream come true!

When she emerged from the caravan, she stumbled as she put her weight on her sore foot, and Silas came forward quickly and grabbed her arm.

"You okay?"

"I'm fine." Eva felt embarrassed. "I don't think I got all the rose briar out of my heel last night."

"What have you got on it?"

"A Band-Aid."

He sent her a derisory look and offered the cake plate. Eva took a piece and bit into it. Carrot cake with cream cheese icing. Delicious. "Did you make this, Fanny?"

"You're funny!" Fanny laughed. "Isn't she, Daddy?"

"I wouldn't say *funny,* exactly," Silas said slowly, choosing a carrot stick from the vegetable tray. "More like *interesting* or *mysterious* or maybe *crazy* for not looking after that infected foot."

"I'm sure it'll be fine," Eva said. "Fanny," she went on briskly, "watch out for Andy. Behind you. Would you like to give him some carrots before he invites himself?"

The donkey was leaning over the table. He'd discovered the open Tupperware container with the vegetables and had already knocked over a glass.

After the cake, Eva thought she could politely leave but when she stood, the pain from her foot shot up her leg and she grimaced, shifting her weight onto her right leg.

"That settles it," Silas said. "Come up to the house. I'll put some antibiotic cream on that."

Eva hesitated.

Was she being foolish? If Doris had a first aid kit, Eva had no idea where to find it. Maybe some antibiotic cream was a good idea."Well, all right. I appreciate your concern. If you really think it's necessary."

"I do," he said.

Ten minutes later, Eva sat in the large, dim, old-fashioned but well-equipped kitchen and looked around. She felt rather self-conscious sitting there all by herself with her bare foot in a basin of steaming water. Silas had drawn the water, put a handful of salt in it and then disappeared down the hall. A clock on the wall ticked softly. The counters, a mid-century speckled grey Arborite pattern, were spotless and the porcelain-and-brass pump handle by the huge stainless steel sink gleamed. The kitchen was shipshape.

A door slammed somewhere and a few seconds later, Fanny and Bruno entered the room. "Is my dad fixing your foot yet?"

Eva bobbed her foot in the water. "I guess so."

She wished now that she hadn't let Silas talk her into coming inside the house. An infected splinter was hardly a life-threatening injury.

"Is the water *real* hot?"

"Yes." Eva smiled and lifted her foot, which was quite pink already. She wiggled her toes. Where was Silas with the first aid cream he'd promised?

"Did you like my party?"

Eva nodded. "It was lovely. Thank you for inviting me—"

"I made the 'vitations myself," Fanny interrupted. Her eyes glowed.

"You did a beautiful job."

"I did, didn't I?" she agreed.

"Oh, my goodness! No one told me you were here." An older woman, obviously the housekeeper, came in through a side door. "You must be the young lady staying in the house on the other side."

Eva extended her hand awkwardly. "I'm Eva Haines. Doris is a cousin of my mother's."

"I see. So she's your second cousin then?"

"Yes."

"I'm Agnes Klassen." Mrs. Klassen put a knitting bag on the table and bustled toward the stove. She glanced at the hall and lowered her voice. "How is she, by the way?"

"Doris?"

The housekeeper nodded. "I don't know her well,

of course, just to say hello if I saw her shopping or whatnot on the mainland, but I do know she had a bad spell earlier this spring.''

''She broke her hip but she's doing quite well now. She's in a nursing home in Sechelt. Seaview Lodge.''

''Is she? I'm glad to hear it,'' the older woman said hastily, then glanced again at the doorway to the hall. ''You'll have a cup of tea?'' she continued in a normal tone.

''Oh, no, thank you,'' Eva said. ''I'm just on my way—'' She looked helplessly at her foot, immersed in the rapidly cooling water. ''I'm just—''

''She's got a sore foot, Auntie Aggie,'' Fanny explained. ''My dad's gonna fix it up.''

''Silas should have told me you were here. Honestly!'' The elderly housekeeper settled into a rocking chair by the window with her knitting. She took out a small piece, yellow, with blue ducks knitted into the yoke of what looked very much like the back of a child's cardigan. The color was suspiciously familiar.

The clack-clack of the knitting needles filled the silence for a long minute. Eva desperately wished again that she'd just gone home. ''Are you here for the summer?'' she asked, casting about for something—*anything*—to say.

The housekeeper raised her head abruptly. ''No,

we've been here, me and my husband, for nearly three years now.'' She sighed. ''This latest time, anyway. I worked for Silas's parents before, too, you know. Here and at their place in West Vancouver. That would be some years ago, of course.''

''I see.'' So Fanny and her father—and the Klassens—really were living on the island year-round. What did one do here in the winter? ''It must be lonely.''

''Sometimes.'' Mrs. Klassen shook out a strand of yarn from her work bag. ''Oh, but there's always something to do and I go over to the mainland regular to visit our son—goodness, child, what are you after now?''

Fanny had opened the refrigerator door and was inspecting the contents. ''I wish we had some of that fizzy water like Eva has in her fridge. Or pop.''

''So you've had a look in our guest's fridge, have you, you nosy little dickens, you?'' the housekeeper asked with a cheerful smile. ''Come here, honey, I want to measure this on you again.''

The girl went obediently to the window, carrying a juice box, and stood quietly while Mrs. Klassen fussed with the garment, pulling and pushing until it fit, in a manner of speaking, on the child's back, over her T-shirt.

''There! Thank you, dear.'' The housekeeper flopped the piece she was working back to front and began on a purl row. It had been years since Eva had knit anything. Her mother had taught her. She'd knit a pair of slippers for Girl Guides, once. And a scarf as a Christmas gift for her sister Kate.

The Newfoundland's sudden focus on the hall entrance alerted Eva to Silas's return. He carried a towel and a handful of first aid supplies, including the tube of ointment he'd gone for.

"How's the foot?"

"It's fine, really. I feel rather foolish going through all this just for a sliver...."

"You can't be too careful. We're on an island here with no doctors, no nurses, no medical help of any kind. It's best to avoid emergencies."

"This isn't an emergency," Eva insisted.

"No. But if your foot had become badly infected, it could be. Would you have come to us for help?" His eyes, a stormy-sea-color, not blue, not green, were intent on her.

"My cousin managed," Eva grumbled, realizing she was being difficult and not exactly sure why.

"Did she?" Silas's look was challenging as he hunkered down in front of her and held out the towel. Obediently she raised her foot and he dried it gently.

"Yes. She was airlifted off, you know. She was a very resourceful woman. She used her cell phone to call for help."

"Did she?" Silas repeated, not meeting her eyes. "So you're related to Doris Bonhomme—"

"I'm her second cousin."

"Sounds like you admire her."

"I do," Eva retorted hotly, realizing she'd just answered the questions Silas had posed in the orchard. "I've always admired her independence. I think she's a wonderful woman."

He said nothing, just inspected her heel carefully. Eva tried hard to squelch her automatic response, which was to either curl up her toes or wrench her foot away altogether. There was something so—so intimate about Silas handling her bare foot, although his touch was as impersonal as any doctor's.

"There's some infection here but it looks as though the hot water has drawn it out. Nothing serious." He ran the towel over the area and Eva frowned.

"Does it hurt?"

"Not really."

"It tickles, Dad!" Fanny said, coming up behind her father and throwing her arms around his neck. "That's what!" There they were together, their faces side by side, his lightly tanned, hers the color of milk chocolate, her impish features alight as she grinned at Eva over her father's shoulder, her dark riot of curls blending with his sun-bleached, tawny hair.

"You should've told me we had company, Silas." The housekeeper's tone was accusing.

"She didn't come to visit us, Aggie. She came to Fanny's party." His cool gaze made the distinction very clear.

"Perhaps she'd like to stay for dinner?" Mrs. Klassen shook out another strand of yarn, her eyes darting between Eva and Silas.

"We made pie!" Fanny crowed, from her position behind her father's back.

"Oh, thank you, but no," Eva said, before the invitation was withdrawn, as she could see from Silas's expression that it might very well be. She didn't want to embarrass the housekeeper, nor did she want to be spoken about as though she wasn't sitting right there in the Lord kitchen. Now she was feeling more like the dormouse than Alice at the Wonderland picnic. "I need to go home and—"

"Here. Let me put this stuff on." Silas squeezed some white gunk from the tube he'd brought onto a small square bandage and placed it over her injury. Eva pulled her foot away as soon as he was finished and fumbled for her sock.

"Kiss it better, Dad!"

Eva reached for her shoe, unable to look up.

"That just works for little girls, Fanny," her father said smoothly.

Fanny clung to his back. "Oh, please, Daddy,

can't Eva stay—'' Then she screamed as her father stood abruptly, leaving her dangling, skinny legs flailing as she sought to keep her grip around his neck. Eva could see that Silas was ready to grab her if necessary, that he had no intention of letting her fall. ''You heard the lady, Fanny. She says she needs to go home. Maybe another time.''

He was only being polite. A strange man. Full of contradictions. One minute he was solicitous, the next he was booting her out.

Eva stood, testing her weight on her heel. She had to admit her foot felt better. ''Thank you very much,'' she said and he nodded.

''Very nice to meet you, Mrs. Klassen,'' Eva said. The older woman smiled broadly.

''You'll have to try my blueberry pie another time, Eva. If you get lonely over there, you just come over and see me.''

Eva saw that Silas had frowned at his housekeeper and she'd clacked her needles together and returned his look with an almost defiant one of her own.

Eva pushed open the screen door and was relieved to see Andy waiting for her, tearing at the nasturtiums that grew in a flower bed just outside the kitchen. Silas, she observed, noted the donkey's misdemeanor but remained silent.

''Bye, Eva!'' Fanny called, from her piggyback position on her father's shoulders.

Eva waved. "Goodbye, Fanny. You're welcome to visit me anytime." She, too, gave Silas a defiant look.

His expression was cool. "How long are you staying?" Again the questions!

"Another week or so. Two at most." Eva paused, again recalling Silas's questions in the orchard. She might as well tell him.... "I'm clearing up my cousin's affairs here. Closing down her house."

"Please feel free to go on using The Baths while you're here," Silas said quietly. "There's a small cabana near the hemlock tree, which you're welcome to use. Maybe you hadn't noticed it."

"Thank you." She dared to meet his gaze, her heart pounding. "I hadn't."

Eva walked swiftly toward the path that led first to the small, well-stocked harbor, where she'd seen a runabout, as well as a good-size cruiser, a small sailboat and a floatplane, then led toward the Bonhomme property.

He'd seen her! Swimming naked! She was never, *ever* going to The Baths again!

CHAPTER SEVEN

AFTER BREAKFAST, Eva decided to start a fire in the old stone fire pit in the garden, the happy scene of many wiener roasts in the past. It was a good burning day, with not a breath of wind, and she wanted to start getting rid of some of the trash she'd accumulated going through Doris's things. Old wrapping paper and string, discarded furniture piled in the woodshed, old but not collectible magazines and ancient foodstuffs, like jelly powder and macaroni dinner, years past their "best by" dates. Yellowed receipts for purchases of thirty and forty years ago, incomplete decks of playing cards, jigsaw puzzles in broken boxes.

Sorting through someone else's life was fascinating. Eva found herself trying to reconcile the Doris Bonhomme she'd known since childhood with the detritus of the past she was uncovering. So far, there'd been no big revelations, no mysterious keys to safety deposit boxes, no bundles of love letters.

Eva had never thought of herself as much of a romantic, but perhaps she was, for even *thinking* there might be love letters somewhere. Now that she knew a descendant of the Lord family still lived on the eastern half of the island, she was more curious than ever about the original rift between the families.

Silas Lord. Eva's face warmed suddenly and it wasn't from standing too near the flames.

She was no prude. So he'd seen her swimming in her birthday suit. Big deal. He'd probably seen a lot of women with nothing on.

Still, it was embarrassing. She'd gone to The Baths several times when she'd believed she was the only human being on the island. After she'd realized she wasn't, she'd avoided the rock pools and had swum in the ocean directly in front of Doris's house.

How often had he seen her? On the one hand, the information that he'd spied on her made her angry. But at the same time, there was something about his watching her unseen that was—titillating.

And that alarmed her.

Silas Lord was an attractive man. Eva was very definitely not immune. What woman would be? Having him handle her bare foot hadn't helped—heavens, she was starting to think like some love-starved teenager!

Still, her response had surprised her. In a way, her reactions *did* belong to some inexperienced teen. Normally, she was not drawn to men like Fanny's father. There was a hard edge to him that she'd sensed immediately. Dangerous, possibly. Enigmatic, unquestionably. All those personal questions, probing into her reasons for being on the island. Revealing so little about himself. Eva had a few questions, too. Who was Fanny's mother and, more importantly, *where* was she? Eva didn't like unpredictable men; perhaps she'd had too much of it growing up with Jack Haines.

She was annoyed with herself for going over and over what had happened since she'd met Fanny. Was she already developing some kind of "island" mentality? Was this what had happened to Doris over the years, her views hardening and narrowing with too much time on her hands and too little input from the outside world? Eva had been here just over a week and look how she was obsessing about the particulars of her mysterious neighbors!

As she worked, dragging armload after armload of debris into the yard to feed the fire, she gradually stopped thinking about Fanny and her father. At about two o'clock, when she was in the house fixing herself a cup of tea and a snack, she heard a tap on her door.

"Fanny!" The sudden swoop in her midriff told her she'd half expected someone else.

"Dad said I had to knock and not stay too long and bother you."

"You're no bother, honey." Eva held the door wide and Fanny and her dog walked into the kitchen. "I'm just having a snack. Would you like one?"

Fanny put one finger to her lips and frowned. "Hmm. That depends. What have you got?"

Eva laughed. "Cookies and crackers and cheese and apples. I'm having an apple and some cheese." Fanny's response reminded her of her own childhood. An invitation to a friend's for dinner always resulted in speculation about the menu. If a favorite such as spaghetti was on offer at one household, that was usually where she and her friend ended up, regardless of the original invitation. At that age, what was on the menu was always more important than the people with whom you dined.

"What kind of cookies?"

"Chocolate chip."

"Yes, please!"

Eva carried their snacks out to the back patio where she could keep an eye on the fire. The flagstone-paved patio was built in the ell between the two-story portion of the house and the one-story multiwindowed music room and living room portion. Eva often ate her meals on the patio in the shade of the evergreen clematis that climbed over the bamboo pergola. With no wind today, there was little danger of sparks, but Eva had several buckets of water near the stone-rimmed fire pit, just in case.

"What are you burning—garbage?" Fanny clambered up onto one of Doris's old wrought-iron chairs and reached for her cookie and the glass of lemonade plus sparkling water Eva had poured for her. "Uncle Matthew burns our garbage in a barrel by the orchard."

"I'm getting rid of some of my cousin's old stuff," Eva replied. "Junk."

"I *like* junk. Can I see some of her junk?"

"Sure." Eva gave the child a smile. Fanny liked everything. "You can sort through her old jewelry, how about that? That'd be a big help to me. Pick out what you'd like to keep and I'll take the rest to the thrift store."

Fanny played happily with Doris's costume jewelry, most of it worthless, for an hour or so, while Eva tended the fire, tossing on articles as she found them. Two torn roller blinds from an upstairs bedroom—if the marine park people were going to use this house for a caretaker, they would doubtless refurbish it from top to bottom—picture frames with no pictures, a dilapidated wicker sewing basket, several sun-faded lampshades with no lamps, an entire drawerful of carefully folded paper grocery bags. Doris hadn't discarded anything that she thought might "come in handy" someday.

When she tired of the jewelry, Fanny joined Eva outside and settled down on one corner of the patio to sort through a stack of old magazines, looking for pictures to cut out, while her dog snoozed under the arbutus tree. Eva had just pushed the embers of the dying fire together in the center, thinking it was about time to call it a day, when Bruno got to his feet and started wagging his tail, ambling toward the patio. Eva turned.

"I knocked but no one answered. So I walked around." Silas was standing on the grass by the corner of the house. He wore bathing trunks and a white T-shirt and held a red-and-white striped bag in one hand.

"Daddy!" Fanny looked up from her cross-legged position on the flagstones. "See all the pictures Eva gave me? I'm helping her. And she said I'm no bother at all."

Silas smiled and Eva felt an odd little jab somewhere under her ribs, the same kind of jolt she'd had when she'd seen him at Eva's party yesterday. "Time for our swim, princess. Perhaps you'd like to join us?" He addressed Eva, sunglasses angled up onto his forehead, his eyes directly on her.

"Me?" Eva looked down at her dusty shorts and T-shirt. She was a mess. Even her hair had to be full of cobwebs. But she wanted to accept his offer....

"It's a hot afternoon," he said. "Fanny and I usually go for a swim about now."

"Out here?" Eva indicated the harbor in front of Doris's house with a wave of one hand. But of course not—they'd swim at their end of the island somewhere.

"No," he replied evenly. "We usually go to The Baths."

Eva had the impression that he was issuing a challenge. How could she possibly refuse? She was no coward and besides, a dip sounded wonderful. She'd show him that his reference to seeing her bathing nude hadn't rattled her in the least.

"I've got Fanny's suit in here," he continued, holding up the canvas bag. "You two can change in the cabana, if you want."

Eva retrieved her bathing suit from the rack in the kitchen and ducked into the bathroom for a towel.

When she left the house, Silas and Fanny had already started down the path. Bruno, as usual, was right beside Fanny, who skipped along a few steps ahead of her father. He turned and put on his sunglasses as Eva closed the door behind her.

Eva wished she'd brought hers. She hated the idea that she couldn't see his expression as clearly as he could see hers. She adjusted the brim of her sun hat, shading her face.

"How's the foot?"

"Fine." Eva glanced up. "Thanks." She was sure it would have been equally fine without his ministrations, but she didn't want to seem ungrateful. And, indeed, she appreciated his concern.

"I hope Fanny hasn't been a nuisance," he said.

"Not at all. I enjoy her company." They were going up the small rise that formed the spine of the island. "She's probably lonely—"

"I don't think so," he interrupted brusquely. "She has the run of the island and there are plenty of things to do here. She's just curious about you, that's all."

"Yes," Eva agreed noncommittally. *Lonely, just like I said…*

The path they were on veered to the right before they reached the largest and deepest of the pools, the one Eva preferred. They came out above the second of the three, a slightly smaller pool with a stone ledge rimming the water, making for easier access. The first pool, closest to the open water, was the shallowest. A child could walk across it, even at high tide, when it was contiguous with the other ones. During low tide—as at present—the pools were separated by a bridge of sandstone.

"The cabana's over there." Silas handed Fanny the striped bag and pointed toward a large hemlock tree at the top of the rise, not far from the path. "Fanny will show you where it is."

He stripped off his T-shirt. Eva glimpsed a deeply tanned, firmly muscled back, and then Silas was gone, diving cleanly into the dark, still water. Bruno followed him, plunging off the sandstone ledge and heading toward his master, who emerged at the far side of the pool, shaking wet hair out of his eyes.

"Come on!" Fanny led the way, up some steps worn into the lichen on the rocks, to the cabana, striped green-and-orange canvas hanging from crosspieces suspended from a big branch of the hemlock.

The girl immediately stripped and put on her suit, a frilly purple-and-pink affair, and then left, urging Eva to hurry.

Eva had brought a navy Speedo today, a plain utility suit. Nevertheless, she was very conscious of Silas's gaze when she emerged from behind the hemlock and began to make her way down to the water.

He was playing with Fanny, tossing her into the air and letting her fall, shrieking, into the water. Bruno swam this way and that between them, barking occasionally and whining.

Eva felt sorry for the big black dog. He spent his days—and probably nights—beside the little girl, looking out for her, protecting her. The breed's instincts for lifesaving in the water ran bone-and-sinew-deep. The Newfoundland had no way of knowing that Fanny's cries were shrieks of joy and she was having the time of her life. Eva felt a twinge of pain. Had Jack Haines ever played with his daughters so freely, so wholeheartedly? Perhaps he had with Kate and Leona.

"Come on in, the water's fine!" Silas yelled.

A cliché. Eva hesitated. She liked to get in gradually, maybe go knee-deep, wait a few minutes, then take the next step. It was hard to do at The Baths. At this pool, the sandstone ledge fell off fairly steeply, but at least she didn't have to jump right in as Silas had.

"Look at me, Eva!" Fanny was being towed around the pond hanging on to Bruno's collar.

"Look at me, Eva!" Silas launched himself toward her with a few powerful strokes and Eva jumped in out of plain fear. She didn't want to be splashed—or worse, grabbed, pulled in....

"Ooh!" she gasped. The water wasn't really that cold, warmed as it was by the sun over the course of the tide change each day, but it always seemed cold on sun-heated skin.

To Eva's relief, Silas veered back toward Bruno and his daughter as soon as Eva jumped in. Joining them for a swim was one thing, but she wasn't here to fool around in the water with them, as though they were old friends.

She was here to cool off and have a wash. It

turned out they all were. After splashing around for another ten minutes or so, Silas and Fanny got out of the water and Eva watched as Silas dug something out of the canvas bag he'd left on the stone ledge. He began lathering his daughter's hair.

Darn! She'd forgotten to bring her soap and shampoo. Eva swam several more lengths, then got out, a few yards away from Silas and Fanny. She was hoping to avoid Bruno's enthusiastic shakes, but he trotted over and included her before she could grab her towel for protection.

"Want some?" Silas held up a cloth and the bar he was wielding. "This is a shampoo bar."

"Thank you." Eva decided she might as well, and walked toward them. "I meant to bring mine but I forgot."

"There's always some in the cabana," he said. "Want me to do your back?"

"No, thanks." Eva looked at him sharply. His tone was calm and friendly, but his eyes were gleaming with amusement. "I'll borrow it to do my hair, though."

She quickly sudsed her hair, intending to rinse the salt out when she got home. With unreliable plumbing and little hot water at Doris's house, Eva often bathed this way, had done since she was a child. So did Silas and his daughter, obviously.

Afterward, they sat on the sun-warmed sandstone

ledge, drying off and soaking up the heat. Silas spread out beach towels and pulled a paperback out of his bag. Bruno, of course, performed his last thorough shake right next to Fanny and she squealed.

"Sunscreen?" Silas glanced at Eva.

Eva shook her head. "I'm going in a few minutes."

"Put some on me, Dad!" Fanny demanded, turning onto her stomach.

Obediently, he slathered sunscreen on his daughter's back and skinny calves as she lay, facedown, on a Mickey Mouse towel.

"You're sure?" Silas held up the tube of sunscreen when he'd finished with his daughter.

"Thanks, but no," Eva said quickly, getting to her feet and tossing back her damp hair. His gaze followed her gesture. Was he offering the sunscreen—or his services applying it, too?

Eva felt a little breathless, and not from the dip in the ocean. She was annoyed with herself.

"What's the rush? Andy expecting you?" he murmured. He replaced the top on the sunscreen, tucked it in his bag and picked up his book. Then he lay back on his own beach towel, resting his head on one arm.

Eva wouldn't respond to that, of course. She bent to gather up her towel.

"Bye, Fanny," she said to the girl as she folded her towel. "See you another time."

"But?" The child frowned accusingly at her father.

"Oh, yes! Aggie wants to know if you'd care to have dinner with us this evening."

Eva didn't know what to say. "Well, thank you, but—"

"Hey, no big deal." Silas held up his hand. "Just show up about six if you decide to join us." Eva couldn't make out his expression, with the dark glasses on. "You'd be very welcome," he finished stiffly, then flipped the page of his book. Sure didn't sound like it!

Eva fought with herself all the way home. No, she wasn't going to the Lords for dinner.

Yes, she was. Why not? She had nothing planned for her own meal beyond the usual can of soup and a sandwich, tuna or grilled cheese or peanut butter.

No, she wasn't going. She had plenty to keep her occupied and there was no point in getting too close to her neighbors, anyway. They were weird.

Why not go? She'd be leaving in less than two weeks if she was fortunate enough to find a home for Andy and finish clearing up Doris's things, and that would be that.

So?

Eva knew she was going to change her clothes

and walk over to the Lords' house for dinner. She was dying to learn more about Fanny and her father. And the Klassens. And the mysterious missing person—Fanny's mother. Eva hadn't missed the lack of enthusiasm in Silas's invitation, either, which also intrigued her.

She was curious, pure and simple. Curiosity was a perfectly good reason to accept a dinner invitation, no matter how reluctantly offered.

Aggie wants to know if you'd care to join us....

Indeed.

CHAPTER EIGHT

SILAS HEARD the slam of the screen door in the kitchen, then the soft murmur of voices. So she'd decided to come, after all. He wasn't sure what he thought of that. He knew he'd wanted her to, and that bothered him. He put down the book he'd been reading and turned to gaze out the window of the music room.

The sun was low but still bright, dappling the yard through the big arbutus and cedar trees that screened the old house from the harbor. The wind had come up half an hour ago, bringing the perfumed heat of the salal and blackberry leaves, as well as the cool of the sea through the open screens and he wondered if a weather change was coming.

Women talking.

Idly, he listened to the rise and fall of the female voices, muffled by distance. It was a pleasant sound that brought back many memories. Silas had always enjoyed the company of women. *Maybe, sometimes, too much.*

Where was Fanny? He was worried about Fanny.

Now that she'd gone over to the other side of the island, against his orders, and met the visitor, there'd be no stopping her. Eva was right; his daughter *was* lonely. These were hellish circumstances. Unable to leave Liberty Island with her for fear of being recognized, he was keeping her here with Matthew and Aggie, where she had just her imagination—and a dog—for company.... But what could he do? A movement by the hedge caught his eye. A double row of topped cedars separated the orchard, which straggled toward the promontory, from the house and yard.

Matthew Klassen came into sight, carrying a rake and a bucket. Fanny skipped along behind, followed inevitably by the ever patient, always-on-duty Bruno. Silas had owned several of the breed, including Bruno's mother, the faithful Althea. She'd lived a long, full life, mostly on Liberty Island, where she was happiest, in and out of the water every day. Bruno was from her final litter. Silas still missed Althea. He'd trust any of her pups with his life—or, even more precious, his child's life. But a child needed more than a dog for a companion.

Matthew had probably been hilling potatoes. Every spring since they'd been back, the Klassens insisted on planting a big vegetable garden. Silas was more than happy to buy everything they needed at Half Moon Bay or Sechelt but he admitted he was glad of the summer greens that appeared regularly on the table, with no effort on his part. And Fanny loved helping in the garden. She especially loved picking radishes, although she'd rarely eat one.

His daughter was utterly smitten with the visitor, he'd realized that afternoon at The Baths. He worried that Fanny would get too attached to someone with whom there could be no contact once she left the island. Why not invite one of the Klassens' great-nieces for a week, as he'd done a few times before? Provide a companion for Fanny, take the pressure off? Silas was always torn. To give Fanny as natural an upbringing as possible under the strange circumstances, or to continue as they'd done the last couple of years, teaching her himself, relying on fly-in trips here and there, to up-coast areas like Prince Rupert and Bella Coola. Hardly the centers of the cultural universe, granted, but excursions that the two of them always enjoyed. Camping, fishing, spending time together.

His mind returned—as it seemed to, these days—to the Eva Haines problem. Two weeks, if that was how long she'd be here, was a long time in a child's world, if Fanny was going to be traipsing over there every day. He couldn't stop her. He didn't *want* to stop her.

It wasn't just because she'd befriended Fanny, although that was a potentially thorny problem in itself. Fanny liked to talk, understandably, and an intelligent woman like Eva was bound to put two and two together, wonder what he and his daughter were doing hidden away on Liberty Island.

No matter how he tried, Silas could not shut her presence out of his mind, even when he was working. It was unsettling.

He was intrigued by Doris Bonhomme's young cousin. More than that, drawn to her. Hell, strongly *attracted.* She wasn't gorgeous. Most men would not consider her beautiful, although to him she was. How much had he been influenced by that fantastic first glimpse through the trees ten days ago, her body suspended in the emerald-dark water, pale, fluid and utterly one with nature? That aside—and Silas thought he *could* put that image aside—there was something more, something intangible about the visitor herself that…

Intangible! Silas knew what lay behind her attraction for him. *Sex.* It was a long time since he'd been in a relationship with a woman. This self-imposed isolation was not natural, in many, many ways.

That was it.

Silas congratulated himself on his analysis. He was a normal, healthy male whose appetites had been suppressed due to his unusual circumstances, living year-round on a remote island off the coast of British Columbia. Knowing that made it easier to do what he had to do: be pleasant but not encouraging. Gracious, but cool. If Fanny hadn't discovered the visitor, he'd have ignored her presence altogether—unless, of course, it looked as though she was planning to stay.

But she wasn't. She was clearing out the Bonhomme place and leaving. Excellent. She'd burned up old rubbish. She was packing boxes. He couldn't have asked for more, considering how irritating he'd always found the old woman's presence. The stupidity of pretending that she wasn't there, all the while keeping an eye on her. Now, with her settled into the Seaview Lodge in Sechelt, he didn't have to think about her anymore. Now he had her cousin to think about.

Since the young, beautiful cousin was a temporary nuisance, Silas's course was clear. Polite distance. Maybe he should offer to help—speed up the process so she could leave even earlier. Maybe spend one week here instead of two. The alternative—seduce her at once and make the most of this serendipitous two weeks—was unthinkable. An enormous temptation, yes, but impossible. Outrageous. Unconscionable.

And there was that other, longer term problem he needed to keep in front of him, the need to protect Fanny from the prying eyes of the outside world.

For just a while longer, until he could figure out what to do next….

A dangerous thought kept entering Silas's mind. Maybe *Eva* was the answer to his prayers. Fanny liked her. He was strongly attracted to her and believed she was attracted to him. He could read the signs. Ordinarily, Silas didn't hold much with the idea of fate, preferring to engineer his own, but didn't it seem as though fate, in the form of Doris Bonhomme's broken hip, had brought Eva to Liberty Island?

To him?

Eva Haines appeared to be a calm, sensible woman. Compassionate. Rational. Unattached. Someone who could be appealed to, if necessary, to understand his predicament, how crucial it was to keep Fanny hidden. She was a teacher—elementary, too.

In every way…*perfect.*

But no. The best strategy—the *safest*—was to do nothing. Involve no one else, especially a smart woman like her who was almost certainly going to ask questions. Wave goodbye to her in a week. Sayonara—only he wouldn't be seeing her again. For three long years he'd kept Fanny safe on Liberty Island. He could manage the situation for another week or two.

Now…how much longer could he put off going

into the kitchen to put his prudent hands-off plan into action?

"Dad!" Silas heard small footsteps running down the hall. Fanny and Matthew had entered the house via the kitchen door. "Dad! Guess who's here? Eva!"

Too excited to wait for his answer, Fanny jumped up and down, her eyes sparkling.

"You run upstairs, honey, and wash up." Silas ruffled his daughter's curls. Difficulties aside, he was deeply gratified to see how happy Fanny'd been the last few days. How *alive.* That was Eva's influence. "Maybe even change your clothes, okay?"

"And she's wearing a *dress!*"

Silas walked quietly down the hall toward the kitchen. Eva and Aggie were both bent over the sink, which was full of lettuce. Eva was laughing at something Aggie had said, her hand resting lightly on the housekeeper's shoulder, and Silas could tell from the way Eva's loosely coiled hair lay at her nape, heavy and dark, that it was still damp from the afternoon's swim.

How long since he'd seen a woman in a dress? Of course, Aggie wore dresses; Silas had never seen her in anything else. But Mrs. Klassen's dresses didn't count. Eva's was plain, sleeveless. An ordinary sundress. A sun color, too, the faded apricot of a Tuscany fresco, splashed with white flowers—daisies, perhaps.

Amber. He could see her in Mexican amber and hammered silver, coolness and mystery against the polished honey of her skin....

Silas shook his head, impatient with himself. He needed a weekend in the city. "Time for me to start the barbecue yet?"

It was just after six.

"OH, SILAS!" Aggie swung toward the hallway, wiping her hands on her apron. "Look what Eva brought us!"

Eva wished Aggie wouldn't make such a big deal of the handful of flowers she'd brought, the jacksonii clematis that was just coming into bloom on Doris's woodshed. Admittedly, the spiky purple flowers did look rather elegant in the cut-glass vase she'd found on a top shelf of a kitchen cupboard, reprieved from the thrift store. The bottle of Perrier, also on the table, was for Fanny, since the girl was so fond of "fizzy" lemonade. Eva wished she'd had a few cans of pop to bring instead.

"Very nice," Silas agreed. "I'll get started, shall I?"

Eva didn't think he'd even glanced at the flowers.

"I'm very fond of flowers," Aggie went on, then stopped, her hands full of lettuce suspended over the sink. ‘‘Come to think of it, I don’t know what’s been after my nasturtiums lately.’’ She shook her head. ‘‘Must be the deer!’’

Silas’s eyes met hers briefly, and Eva was sure she detected a glimmer of amusement before he went out the kitchen door. Eva hoped the guilty party, Andy, had trotted back home after accompanying her most of the way to the Lord house.

‘‘Can I help you with anything, Mrs. Klassen?’’

‘‘Oh, *do* call me Agnes. We’re neighbors now!’’ The housekeeper beamed. ‘‘Yes, I wouldn’t mind if you sliced up these cucumbers and put them into the salad while I take a peek at the ribs. I’ve started them in the oven. Or would you rather wash this lettuce Matthew just brought in? I always tell him, please, *not* right when I’m getting a meal ready, but does he ever listen? He sees it, he picks it....’’

The housekeeper’s voice was muffled slightly as she disappeared into the pantry and emerged tying a fresh apron around her ample middle. ‘‘But then isn’t that just like a man?’’

Eva made some soothing noises. Mrs. Klassen had been ecstatic when she’d shown up, bearing flowers and Perrier. No matter what she’d said the day before, it was clear the older woman was lonely.

Agnes Klassen appeared to be well into her sixties. Her husband, Matthew, a long, thin, silent type with an Adam’s apple that bobbed around like soap on a rope, appeared to be even older. He'd smiled shyly when Agnes had introduced them and extended a large-knuckled work-worn hand. Then he'd gone out again.

These people were too old to be taking care of Silas and his little daughter. They should be retired and living in a cottage by the sea somewhere. As Eva and her sisters had once imagined, Silas, like his grandfather, seemed to have "pots" of money. Between the three boats and the seaplane, there had to be several hundred-thousand dollars worth of transportation moored at the Lord dock. He could easily afford younger, more able caretakers.

And why had Fanny said the other day that she wished she could go to school, like kids in books? What did it all *mean?*

Eva followed the housekeeper out to the big, new-looking deck at the back of the house. Silas was standing over a propane barbecue and Matthew was just approaching from around the corner of the house. He'd changed his shirt and removed his overalls and his hair looked freshly dampened and combed in furrows. A table, already laid with a cloth, plates and cutlery, was set up under the trees. With the glint of the water a brilliant blue in the distance, beyond the gently undulating green branches of the big birch and arbutus trees forming an arch above the table, Eva could not have imagined a more perfect picnic setting. After all her dithering, she was very glad she'd decided to accept the invitation to dinner, no matter how reluctantly forwarded.

"There you go!" The housekeeper passed an open graniteware roaster to Silas, who set it on a table by the barbecue. "You can finish these ribs on the grill," she directed, "and Eva and I will bring out the rest."

There was a green salad and a potato salad, bristling with hard-boiled eggs, radishes and green onions; jugs of water and juice; crusty rolls which had been warmed in the oven; butter in a glass-lidded dish set upon a bowl of crushed ice; and a divided platter containing two kinds of pickles and stuffed olives. A nice change from canned soup and sandwiches.

Where was Fanny?

As though reading her thoughts, the child emerged from French doors that led from another room, toward the east. The living room? Eva had only been in the kitchen area of the house.

"Ta-da!" The girl moved lightly down the stone steps like the princess her father called her, dressed in a frilly red dress and holding her skirt wide. She minced toward the picnic area, twirling from time to time, putting on a display for the adults. Eva clapped her hands and stifled a smile. The princess had running shoes on.

CHAPTER NINE

FANNY RAN straight to Eva. Silas felt a hard jab in his chest as the woman and the girl smiled at each other. The electricity in the air literally hummed, set the leaves aflutter. Couldn't the Klassens feel it? Silas glanced at them; they both wore their doting smiles and were watching Eva and the child with obvious pleasure. Aggie clapped, too, and Silas would've sworn he heard her "Yippee!"

Eva must have sensed his dismay. She gestured toward him. "Show your father, Fanny." Fanny took a step in his direction and obediently twirled again. Aggie laughed, and even Matthew smiled broadly.

"See me, Daddy? I'm pretending I'm a dancer!"

"I see you, princess." *Vivian had been a dancer.* The dress Fanny had on was one he'd bought her on a trip to Chicago that spring. He'd given the woman in the shop her measurements and a wad of money and she'd picked it out. Fanny never wore the dresses he gave her, except for playing dress-up or for one of her parties with Bruno and her dolls.

Of course, where could she wear a pretty dress on Liberty Island?

Eva beckoned and when Fanny returned, spoke softly to her as she bent down and refastened the front of the red dress—Silas had noticed that Fanny hadn't gotten the buttons done properly—and straightened the wide white collar, smoothing it over her shoulders. Then she framed the girl's face with both hands for a few seconds, smiled, and pushed the tangle of curls aside. "*Now* go see your father. Do one of your fancy twirls for him."

Fanny ran up onto the deck, waggling her fingers high in the air as she came toward him. She managed a turn on one foot, laughing, then Silas stepped forward and scooped her up. He lifted her above his head, marveling, as always, at how much love and energy was bound up in this featherweight wiry child. She shrieked with mock fear and laughter, then he kissed her loudly several times and set her down. Bruno wagged his tail and came to Silas's knee for some attention. He tousled the big dog's ears, then pushed him away.

"Okay." Silas took a deep breath. He grabbed a pair of tongs and began transferring sizzling meat from the grill to the platter Aggie had supplied. "Who's ready for ribs?"

"Ribs?" Fanny's expression was comical. "I thought we were having *hot* dogs!"

Aggie threw up her hands. "Oh, for heaven's sake! Where's my mind today? How could I have forgotten the hot dogs?"

It was nearly half past seven by the time they'd finished their meal. Then came ice cream and raspberries from the garden. Aggie brought out tea and Eva cleared away the food, and the two women sat under the trees in lawn chairs, Aggie knitting and Eva watching. Silas stayed at the table with his tea, opposite Matthew, and eavesdropped on the desultory conversation among the three females. He watched as Fanny clambered up on Eva's knee for a while, sucking her thumb, as she often did when she was tired. She slithered down and sat on the ground, leaning against the Newfoundland. From time to time, Silas would catch Matthew's eye and they'd share a male moment. Good humor. Surprise. Incomprehension.

There was some book about men being from Mars and women from Venus. Mostly, he didn't believe that, but sometimes he couldn't understand what women went on about. It was good to have it confirmed that Matthew, a man he admired and respected, didn't know, either.

"Eva, do you have a mom *and* a dad?" his daughter suddenly asked and Silas felt fear clutch his vitals. *He'd robbed his child of a mother....*

"I have a dad, honey," Eva replied in a low voice

and Silas listened intently. ‘‘He lives near Vancouver. On a houseboat in the Fraser River.’’

‘‘A boat?’’ Fanny gave an artificial laugh, the one she drew on to ‘‘be sociable.’’ ‘‘That's funny! Where's your mom? Is she on a boat, too?’’

There was a slight hesitation, but Silas realized it was because Eva had been moved by his daughter's question, not that she was reluctant to answer. ‘‘My mother's dead, Fanny. She died many years ago, when I was a girl.’’

‘‘As little as me?’’

‘‘No.’’ Eva's smile was sad. ‘‘I was twelve when she died. She had something wrong with her that couldn't be fixed. I miss her a lot. But I have sisters,’’ she continued, making an effort, Silas could sense, to brighten the conversation.

‘‘How many?’’

‘‘Two.’’

‘‘Do they live on boats?’’

Eva laughed, a sound he'd become accustomed to and looked forward to hearing. ‘‘No. They're all grown-up now and they live far away. One lives in Africa and the other lives in Alberta.’’

‘‘Do they have kids?’’ Fanny asked, and Silas wondered if he should interrupt, discourage his daughter from being so nosy.

‘‘Well, my sister in Africa doesn't have any children. But my sister, Leona, the one in Alberta has five.''

''Five!'' Fanny seemed impressed and was quiet for a few moments, digesting this latest bit of information. ''Girls?''

''Two boys and three girls.''

''Everybody has a mommy and daddy, right?''

Eva nodded, looking a little perplexed. Silas held his breath. ''Sure, they do.''

''*Some*where,'' the girl went on earnestly. ''Even if they're dead, like your mommy.'' She paused, then finished firmly, ''Even *I* do.''

Silas exhaled slowly, glad Eva didn't pursue the subject. Fanny's ideas about mothers came from books, as far as he could tell. He was positive she had no real memory of Vivian. He hoped so; it would be easier....

Matthew gave him an odd look, half sympathy, half challenge, over the expanse of the cleared table. ''Well, now, Silas. Would you be wantin' me to start a bonfire this evening?''

''Yeah!'' Fanny got to her feet and began running around under the trees, weaving this way and that, arms spread wide in an airplane impression. Bruno trotted behind her, tongue lolling. ''Yes! Yes, *please!* And—and *marshmallows!*''

Silas had thought that Eva would've left by now. Dinner was over and the sun was very low. He'd found her presence far more stressful than he'd anticipated. *You have a good plan,* he told himself grimly, *stick to it. She'll be gone soon and that'll be the end of that.* Fanny would forget her in a few days. Kids did. Just as Matthew's mention of the bonfire had put all further questions about mommies and daddies out of Fanny's head.

Fanny helped Matthew bring some firewood from the woodshed. She carried kindling. It was a little ritual she shared with the old man. They often lit a fire in the evening—what Fanny called a "campfire"—in the stone pit at the edge of the orchard. It was a good place to watch the sun go down and Aggie was as big a fan of roasted marshmallows as his daughter. The two women wandered toward the fire pit, still talking, while Silas went for lawn chairs.

"I should go home," Eva said softly when he returned. He heard the note of regret. "It's been a lovely evening."

"Glad you came?" He positioned a chair near the fire, which Matthew had started, and gestured for her to take it. Aggie had gone to the kitchen to get marshmallows.

"Yes." She met his eyes. "Yes, I am."

"Are you lonely over there by yourself?" He hadn't meant to blurt that out; it certainly didn't fit with his determination to be civil but distant. But he couldn't help himself. The idea of her spending nights alone in that broken-down old house…

"I hadn't thought so until this evening," she said with a laugh, then added, almost to herself, "Perhaps I am."

"I'll cook a marshmallow for Aggie and Dad can cook one for you, Eva," Fanny said, appearing with several wood-handled pronged tools designed for the purpose. "How about that?"

"Good idea." Silas moved closer to the fire and allowed Fanny to fit marshmallows onto the ends of two prongs while he held them for her. The fire had blazed up quickly and was still too hot, but nothing could deter his daughter, who thrust her marshmallow in the fire and then pulled it out again when it looked like it might catch fire. Silas hunkered down beside her, his back to Eva, and positioned his stick near the flame.

Too close, and it would burn.

After a few minutes, he swung around to offer the perfectly roasted marshmallow to Eva. "Here you go, madam."

She wrinkled her nose. "Ugh," she whispered. "Do I have to?"

"I know what you mean. Absolutely disgusting things. I never eat them myself—"

"Daddy!" Fanny protested, keeping an eye on the marshmallow she was "cooking" for Aggie.

"—but, yes, you must. It's an ancient Liberty Island custom. Careful! Don't burn yourself."

Eva touched the puffy golden marshmallow with one tentative finger. Then she held out her hand and grasped the marshmallow gently between her fingers. Very slowly, he pulled the stick away.

"Ah!" he said. "Things are not as they seem." Her hand held the golden brown outer shell while the white heart of the marshmallow still trembled on the stick.

"Not fair!" She laughed and popped the crust into her mouth, her smiling gaze on him. Silas felt the blood rise in his throat. He wanted to take her hand, raise her to her feet. Put his arms around her. Taste the confection on her lips, draw the sweetness of her mouth to his—

Horrified, he turned back to the fire. He hardly noticed when the pale blob slid off his stick and vanished in the glowing coals.

AS SOON AS THE SUN disappeared completely beneath the horizon, Eva wished, first of all, that she'd gone home an hour ago, but since she hadn't, she wished she'd thought to bring a sweater and a flashlight.

"Chilly?" As though reading her mind, Silas emerged from the darkness behind her holding a cardigan sweater, probably one belonging to Mrs. Klassen. He'd brought his housekeeper a sweater, too, and as he walked over to deliver it, Eva noticed he carried a flashlight.

"I'll take you home," he said when he returned. "Aggie's going to give Fanny her bath and she'll be ready for her story by the time I get back."

"I can walk home by myself," Eva said. "Heavens! It's not far and—"

"I'll go with you," he insisted.

Fine. Eva said her goodbyes and bent to kiss Fanny on the cheek. "Thanks for everything," she whispered. "I had a really good time. Be sure and visit me whenever you like."

Fanny threw her arms around Eva's neck and held on tightly. She was surprisingly strong. "Bye, Eva," she whispered and kissed Eva's cheek.

It was a lot darker than she'd been aware and the wind had come up strongly off the water. She'd been staring into the bonfire, half dreaming, completely unaware of the time. It had to be well past nine already.

She followed Silas around to the other side of the house, the side that faced the Lord harbor to the north. The path dipped down the hill somewhat, veered to the left, then climbed a few feet to continue on the other side of the cove in the general direction of The Baths. Before it reached The Baths, Eva now knew, another narrow trail veered off to the west, eventually emerging at the creek that separated the two properties, not far from Doris's house.

No sign of Andy, of course. He'd probably settled down for the night, already dozing under his favorite tree behind the garden.

"Here, I'll go ahead."

It was awkward walking side by side without bumping into each other on the narrow path and Silas's suggestion made sense. Eva followed closely behind, her left arm raised up to ward off soft branches that might hang over the trail and be disturbed by Silas's progress. *Or spiderwebs. Or bats.* Now that she knew how dark it was, she was actually relieved that Silas had insisted on accompanying her. Not that there was anything to be afraid of on Liberty Island and she'd never been afraid of the dark before.

Matthew could very well have escorted her.

Which would have been a disappointment. Her reaction made her think again about the events of the evening. How generally polite and hospitable Silas had been, how terribly aware of him she'd felt every single second. The definite sense she'd had that he was on guard about something, that he was holding himself in tight control. Why? How many times had she glanced his way only to find that he was watching her? It had frightened her a bit. Made her think that maybe there was some real secret about Silas Lord. Something not quite right. Was he a criminal, hiding out here on Liberty Island? A pirate, she thought wildly, as she and Kate and Leona used to speculate about his grandfather? No, that was ridiculous! Would honest, salt-of-the-earth people like Aggie and Matthew Klassen be mixed up with a criminal or a modern-day pirate. Hardly.

No, maybe what she'd noticed between them was simpler, more primitive. Currents and subcurrents of physical attraction—or not. Just as with the pirate fantasy, chances were she was making this up as she went, kind of an island-induced fancy....

Which brought her back to the issue that had troubled her since she'd met Fanny and her father. "Silas? I wonder if I could ask you a question."

"Yes?" He turned, moving a little off the path so that she could come up beside him.

"Where's your wife?" Eva felt out of breath, no doubt from the rather brisk pace he'd set.

"I don't have a wife."

Had he paused just a shade too long? And why the rush of feeling—relief?—at his answer? He wore no wedding ring, but that meant nothing. "I mean Fanny's mother. Where's Fanny's mother?"

This time she didn't imagine it; he did hesitate for several seconds. "Why do you ask?"

That brought heat to her cheeks. He thought she

was prying. Luckily, in the dark—the flashlight was still pointed down, illuminating the path beneath their feet—he couldn't see her expression. "Fanny clearly misses her mother," she went on doggedly. "I just wondered where she was. I notice that no one talks about her—"

"I don't know where Fanny's mother is," he interrupted bluntly. "That's the whole truth. And I would prefer if you'd avoid the subject with my daughter. As you might imagine, it distresses her."

"What do you mean?" She was astonished at his brusque response to what she thought was a fairly obvious query. "I would never do anything to hurt Fanny! That's why I'm asking you now, privately. Anyone can see that she spends most of her time with adults, that she has no playmates on this island except squirrels and a dog, at least none that I can see, and no mother!"

"My daughter and I have not been abandoned, if that's what you're thinking," he went on grimly, then repeated, "I am not married. Fanny's mother is not my wife. I have never been married. Does that satisfy you?"

"Okay. Fine. Sorry I mentioned it," Eva said, deeply affronted, wrapping her arms around herself in her borrowed sweater. "I just wondered, that's all. I don't think it's an unreasonable question. Can we—can we go on?"

Silas plunged ahead and Eva was hard-pressed to keep up with him. When they got to the creek, he crossed first and reached for her hand when she began to inch out onto the rocks. "Steady," he muttered. "I'm going to have to put some kind of crossing here I guess. Maybe some planks will do...."

"Yes," she said quickly. "It's not as though I'm going to be here long enough to require a bridge."

"No," he agreed, releasing her hand.

"I'm fine now. You can go back. There was really no need for you to come to this side of the creek. But thank you for coming with me," she said stiffly.

"I'll wait until you get a light."

Eva walked toward the house, which loomed dark and brooding on the small knoll. She heard the clatter of hooves on stone in the distance, but couldn't see the donkey.

"Have you ever heard of goats being on this island?" she asked, more to convince herself that she was capable of carrying on an ordinary conversation after the few moments of tension on the trail. Silas Lord didn't frighten her. In fact, she was more curious than ever about his circumstances.

"Yes, I have." They were nearly at her door now. "There's a legend to that effect. I've never seen any goats, though."

He seemed to be trying as hard as she was to continue as though this was just a straightforward end to a social evening, he "dropping her off," and waiting politely until she unlocked her door. Except that she didn't.

"You don't lock your door?" he asked.

"Of course not. There's no one on this island except you and your family and me." Eva felt for the shelf on the wall, to the left of the door, and then for the candle and matches always kept there. "I don't even know if there *is* a lock— Ouch!" The first match she struck flared up unexpectedly, burning her fingers, and she let it drop to the floor. Silas put his foot down quickly on the old linoleum, extinguishing the flame.

"You're going to burn the goddamn house down. Do you want me to light that?"

"No, I don't." She struck a second match and put the flame to the candle wick. It caught immediately.

"Okay?"

"Yes. Thank you and—oh!" She set the candle on the nearby table and began taking off the sweater he'd given her earlier. "Please give this back to Agnes."

He took the sweater, his eyes locked on hers. In the single candle flame, the planes of his face were harsh, a contrast of dark and light, lit from below. "I have something I'd like to ask you."

"Of course." Eva held his gaze steadily. Fair enough. Me, neither—I'm not married, either! some hopelessly immature inner child exulted.

He put one hand up, as though to touch her bare arm, then moved it away. "I was wondering if, well—" He paused and frowned heavily, his eyes burning into hers.

"If *what?*" Eva could barely breathe.

"I was wondering if there was any possibility that your cousin would sell this land to me?"

CHAPTER TEN

EVA SPENT the next day packing boxes. Fanny showed up shortly after lunch, but this time it was Matthew who arrived at four o'clock to take the girl home.

"Your daddy's working, dear. Auntie Aggie and I haven't seen him all day."

It hadn't crossed Eva's mind that Silas worked. Somehow, sweating for one's daily bread had never entered into the "pots" of money scenario. But of course he had to make a living, just as everyone did. "What does Silas do?"

"Oh, my." The old caretaker removed his hat and ran a hand over his tousled gray hair, then replaced the battered panama he always wore. "He does wonderful work with gold and silver and diamonds and precious gems."

Pirate booty, gold and jewels spilling out of thick oaken sea chests and massive porcelain Chinese jars…

"My daddy makes pretty things for ladies, just like the stuff you gave me from the old lady who used to live in this house,'' Fanny said. The day before, Fanny had picked out some of Doris's costume jewelry to use for dress-up. The remainder had already gone into one of the boxes for the thrift shop. ''Sometimes he even lets me put some on. A necklace or something.''

''You mean he's...a jeweler?'' What an astonishing notion!

''Oh, not just any jeweler,'' Matthew answered. ''He does highfalutin stuff for fancy folks. One of a kind, artistic-like. That's his ticket. Come along now, young lady, get your stuff and we'll be on our way.''

Fanny handed Matthew the bulging bag of magazine cuttings she'd collected that afternoon and the day before, and carried the little sack of jewelry herself. Eva watched them leave. String bean of a man wearing an old straw hat, dancing little girl skipping from side to side, huge black dog padding next to them. Andy followed the trio to the creek and then came back.

He nuzzled her hip as she stood just outside the door and she dug around in her shorts pocket, producing half a cookie for him. Then she put her arm around the donkey's grizzled neck and buried her face against his fuzzy ear. It was shocking to admit how disappointed she was that Silas hadn't come for Fanny himself. She realized she'd been looking forward to seeing him all day, perhaps going for a swim again. The fact that he'd sent Matthew showed he had more sense than she did. Especially after the awkwardness of last evening. What in the world was wrong with her?

The next morning, right after breakfast, Eva began trundling boxes down to the wharf in the wheelbarrow. She had a lot to do on the mainland today. Most of the discards were destined for the thrift store affiliated with the local hospital. And it was time she got serious about finding a home for Andy. She'd written out a few notices that she intended to post at various locations: the Half Moon Bay Store, the community bulletin board at Redrooffs Road, the post office in Sechelt and in Gibsons. It wouldn't hurt to put an ad in both local papers, either.

Eva intended to visit Doris, too. She decided she'd run errands throughout the day and join Doris for her dinner at the lodge. Then, if it turned out to be too late to make the boat trip back to Liberty Island, she'd stay at a bed-and-breakfast in Half Moon Bay. She'd seen a sign for a new B and B on Ross Road. Andy wouldn't miss her and the prospect of a luxurious soak in a bathtub with all the hot water she could possibly want was enticing.

No one was expecting her anywhere. On the one hand, it felt rather pleasant to be so independent.

Fancy-free. On the other, it was kind of unsettling, no one knowing—or caring—if she came or went.

Eva had checked the marine weather forecast, and there was no change expected until Sunday, a low moving in from the Queen Charlottes. As she motored steadily away from Liberty Island, she watched Doris's house dwindle and then disappear altogether as she turned east and south, to clear Jedadiah. The Lord end of the island was quiet. No activity that she could see. Of course, the house was situated more to the north, on the other side, facing its own harbor. All the events of the past few days, which had loomed so large in her mind—even caused her some sleepless hours—now seemed the stuff of an overactive imagination. In the hard blue light of midday, in the emerald green of the Strait of Georgia, there was a very visible reminder as she skirted Jedadiah that Liberty Island was just one of many off this coast: Thormanby, Merry, Keats, Trail.

"Hi, there!" Eva tossed a line to a teenage boy who happened to be fishing with a buddy on the floating dock beside the Half Moon Bay wharf. "You boys want to earn a few bucks?"

"Sure!"

Eva had dreaded dragging the boxes all the way up the long wooden stairs that led from the big government wharf, which was on pilings, down to the movable floating dock where the boats tied up. It was low tide, too, which meant an even steeper climb.

''Great! I'll go get my truck and drive it onto the wharf.'' Eva secured the stern line while the boy tied the bow line. ''Why don't you guys just start hauling boxes up and then when I bring the truck around, you can load it. Okay?''

The boys seemed happy to put their fishing rods down for a while. Eva walked to where she'd left her father's Toyota minitruck parked on private property just behind the Half Moon Bay Store, an old-fashioned general store serving the area with everything from kerosene to cappuccino. Eva had paid the property owner a small amount to park her vehicle there for the duration of her stay. It had made sense to swap vehicles with Jack Haines. She needed the cargo space and all he required was something to make the occasional run to the grocery store. Or the liquor store.

Eva's first stop was in Sechelt. She dropped off a dozen boxes of books, sheet music, dishes and knickknacks at the thrift store, as well as several boxes of old clothing. The fancy hats, beaded evening bags and even a forties-style fox fur stole with a rhinestone clasp, would find homes with some drama group or vintage clothing aficionado.

On her way to Gibsons, near the southern end of

the Sunshine Coast, a peninsula accessible to the mainland of British Columbia only by ferry, Eva pondered the wording of her ad. "Elderly donkey needs new home." No, too depressing. "Good home required for sweet-tempered donkey. Free." Should she mention that Andy was free? That might draw too many calls. Plus, maybe weirdos. And she needed to check out any prospects herself, which would take time and energy. No way she wanted Andy going somewhere he'd be neglected or worse.

She reached the *Coast News* office at half-past three and placed her ad, then browsed in the Molly's Lane shops overlooking the harbor for half an hour before heading back up the hill en route to Sechelt again, fifteen kilometers up the coast.

Ah. The Bluebird Bakery. Someone had mentioned it as having great artisan bread and homemade granola. The Half Moon Bay Store had wonderful bread baked by a local lighthouse keeper's wife, but it was usually all sold an hour after it came in and Eva always seemed to miss out.

"Eva, dear!"

"For heaven's sake—Agnes!" Eva couldn't believe she'd run into one of the few people she knew on the Sunshine Coast—in a Gibsons bakery! "What are you doing here?"

"I stop in every Friday when I come down to visit our son," the older woman replied, fumbling as she returned her wallet to her purse. The counter helper was putting a number of loaves of bread into a bag and boxing up a small cheesecake. "I'm just on my way over there now. I always bring Ivor one of the Bluebird's cheesecakes. He's got a sweet tooth, just like his father."

Eva wouldn't have thought so, judging by Matthew's bony physique.

"Are you—alone?" Eva knew Silas wouldn't be with her, nor his daughter, or she'd be in the bakery with Mrs. Klassen.

"Yes. Matthew's home with Fanny, of course. Silas went off to Vancouver this morning early."

"Did he?"

"Yes. He wants to drop in at his studio and—" The housekeeper leaned a little closer. "I think he may have a—a lady friend over there, too. He doesn't tell me everything, of course."

"Of course not."

"Oh, well. He'll be back Sunday. He never goes away for more than a day or two. Too bad it was this morning, though." Mrs. Klassen expertly blew a tendril of graying hair from her perspiring forehead.

"Oh?" Eva couldn't resist some gentle urging. "Why is that?"

"We generally have Ivor every second Friday. He comes back with me and then Matthew or Silas takes him home on the Saturday. That would've been today but Silas suddenly took a notion to go to Vancouver.'' Mrs. Klassen gathered up her baked goods. ''Oh, well. We'll have Ivor next week, I'm sure. His birthday is coming up. Perhaps you could meet him....''

''Here,'' Eva said, stepping forward. ''Let me carry out the cake.''

''Thank you, dear.'' Mrs. Klassen was driving an elderly green station wagon. Eva waved as she left the parking lot, then returned to the bakery to make her own purchase. So Silas had gone to Vancouver....

An hour later, Eva had driven the winding coastal highway north again, past the graveyard where, according to coastal legend, a runaway Danish prince was purported to be buried, past the golf course, past the former hippie enclave of Roberts Creek, past the wide-open beaches of Davis Bay and on to Sechelt, where she submitted her ad to the local weekly, picked up some things she needed from the drugstore and then headed for the nursing home overlooking Trail Bay, where Doris now lived.

It was just past five o'clock, but the residents of Seaview Lodge ate early.

''SO, TELL ME, DORIS, would you ever consider selling your half of the island?'' Eva had decided to broach the subject directly with her cousin. Silas's question two nights ago made sense to Eva. It wasn't a very big island and if he lived there year-round, anyway, why not own the whole thing, if he could afford it?

"What? You mean not turn it over to the marine trust?" Doris's eyes snapped. "Why would I sell it? I don't need the money."

"No." Eva toyed with the ham steak on her plate. "That's true. I just wondered."

They were in the little dining room reserved for residents with guests, a sunny alcove off the main dining room, which had large windows, covered now with blinds to keep out the hot afternoon sun. Flowers graced the tables and low music played on the sound system. Their first course had been a cup of chicken soup, which Eva thought quite tasty and very likely homemade, but which Doris complained loudly was oversalted.

"And who would buy it? No ferry, no roads, no electricity." Doris's eyes probed hers. "Why? Have you had someone express interest?"

"In a way, yes." Eva believed Silas wouldn't have mentioned it if he wasn't seriously interested. She'd told him she'd ask.

"Who?" Doris demanded, leaning forward.

"The man who lives at the other end of the island."

Her elderly cousin's face paled. "Hector?" Her voice was faint.

"Doris!" Eva regarded her quizzically and placed her hand over the older woman's. "Hector Lord has been dead for a very long time. I mean his grandson."

Doris stared at the table for few seconds. "Yes, of course."

When she didn't go on, Eva continued gently. "You should have told me someone was living over there."

Doris didn't appear to be too concerned about the omission. "How did you find out?" She picked up her fork again and poked at her potato salad.

"There's a little girl there. She came over to visit me—"

"A little girl?" Doris seemed astonished. "I wonder who she belongs to?"

"The grandson. It's his daughter. They're living there with an older couple, Agnes and Matthew Klassen."

"Oh, *them!*"

"Don't say that. Agnes is a lovely lady. She enquired about you...."

"She did?" That seemed to spark some interest.

"Yes. She said she'd heard you had an accident and she wanted to know how you were doing."

"Did you tell her?"

"Well, of course I did!" Eva regarded her with some dismay. "How long have you known her? She says she used to see you from time to time, shopping or whatever."

"Oh, I've known of her for years, off and on." Doris sniffed. "Never spoken to her, really. They have that boy who isn't right in his head, you know."

"What's wrong with him?" Eva frowned. It had seemed a little odd the way Mrs. Klassen had spoken of her son, of visiting him every Friday. He had to be a grown man, she'd assumed, possibly with a family of his own.

"Accident. Bunch of boys diving off the rocks at Garden Bay one spring and he got hurt. Brain damage. I'm surprised those two are back with—well, on the island. They bought a little cottage in Hopkins Landing a few years ago to retire and be near their son. Paid too much for it, I heard."

"You're well informed!" Eva smiled and took a sip of water.

"I have my sources," Doris muttered darkly. "When you've lived here as long as I have, you know who's a blabbermouth and who isn't."

"As to exactly why they're on Liberty Island—" Eva had noticed how Doris wouldn't refer directly to Silas Lord or the Klassens as living right next door "—I believe they're helping look after the little girl. There's no sign of the mother."

"Is that so? What about the grandson, what's he like?"

"Oh, very pleasant." *Pleasant?*

"Dark, I suppose? Black hair?"

"Not really. Brownish hair, I think and—" she wrinkled her brow "—fairly tall. Six feet or so."

"Handsome?"

"I would say so," Eva admitted. She wasn't about to tell Doris that Silas Lord had given her some sleepless nights....

"They're all handsome," Doris mumbled. Again, Eva wondered about the feud between the families. Today probably wasn't a good day to ask.

"Andy's doing well," she began, on another note.

"Is he?" Doris didn't seem that concerned, which surprised Eva, as she knew how fond the old woman was of her donkey. "Listen here, Eva. You tell him if you see him again that I would never, ever sell my half of the island to a Lord, not if I didn't have a friend in the world or a penny to my name!"

Eva stared at her. "That seems very unfair, Doris. You don't even know him."

"He's a Lord! And life, my dear, is unfair. Time you learned that." Doris sat back in her chair as one of the servers, a smiling girl with at least six studs in each ear approached to take her half-empty plate. "What's for dessert, pet?"

"Tapioca or apple crisp," the girl said cheerfully, brushing the crumbs from the tabletop.

"Oh, goody!" Doris brightened. "I like tapioca!"

EVA DECIDED to check into a Sechelt motel instead of venturing out onto the strait in the evening. She wasn't worried about her seamanship; it was more a case of not looking forward to returning to an empty house, even emptier now than it had been before the bonfire two days ago and today's shipment of boxes to the mainland. Somehow, being with other people today, even a cranky Doris, had made her reluctant to return to the company of a donkey.

And Silas was away. There'd be no visits from him for a while. Her news for him, when she saw him again, was not hopeful. Doris had been adamant about not selling to anyone, particularly him.

Why was she thinking about Silas so much? She'd only known him a week! She'd had boyfriends. She'd been engaged once, for nearly six months, and she could barely remember what her ex-fiancé looked like. It was crazy. She could see Silas occupying her thoughts while she was on Liberty Island; there wasn't much to do. But here?

She went to a movie at the Raven's Cry Theatre, on the edge of the Sechelt Indian Reserve, which bordered the town, part of an Indian-sponsored commercial development.

Of course, it was a romantic comedy.

She enjoyed a long soak in the motel's bathtub, reading the book she'd brought with her, then shampooed her hair and used the motel's blow dryer—electricity!—intending to repeat the entire operation in the morning before heading for Half Moon Bay, her boat and Liberty Island. What luxury.

Eva got into the queen-size bed and flicked on the television, zipping through the channels for something to put her to sleep.

Talk shows, comedy, sitcoms, police stuff, reality—and another romantic movie, this one an old Rock Hudson and Doris Day film.

Eva turned off the television and switched off her bedside light. Romance definitely wasn't putting her to sleep these days!

CHAPTER ELEVEN

SILAS SET HIS ALARM for half-past five and was untying the Piper Cub at six o'clock. He'd sneaked into Fanny's bedroom before he left the house, as he often did early in the morning, just to look at her. Bruno, naturally, was stretched out on the braided rug at the foot of the bed. He raised his massive head when Silas came in, then sighed and put it down again. Fanny slept soundly with her arm around a favorite teddy bear and her bed covered with stuffed toys. Silas wanted to kiss her but didn't want to chance waking her up.

He hated goodbyes.

He'd call Fanny from the condo after breakfast. If he left now, he'd be landing in Vancouver's Coal Harbour by seven o'clock and tying up the floatplane at the Two Sisters Air docks where he kept a berth. The condo was a twenty-minute walk from there.

There were two Lord condominiums in the Coal

Harbour complex on West Georgia Street—his mother's penthouse and his own two-bedroom suite on the seventeenth floor.

Silas had purchased the condo six years earlier, mostly as an investment. He'd known when he bought it that he wouldn't be living in Vancouver year-round. There were the various business interests he'd taken over from his father about that time and his own career, his passion for using minerals and metals of the earth and crafting them into objects for beautiful women to wear.

Six years. An age. Nothing he'd planned back then, except his year-long trip to Europe to study with the masters of Fabergé, Bugatti and Tiffany, had happened. Instead, he'd met Vivian. He'd put together an award-winning photographic essay with her modeling his best pieces. *He'd fathered a child.*

There was life before Fanny and life after Fanny. Now, as he walked through the early-morning canyons of the downtown high-rises and office towers, he thought about how different the last few years would have been if she hadn't come into his life, and realized that there wasn't anything he would change.

In the condo, a maple-glass-and-steel layout with sleek décor to match, Silas fixed himself eggs, toast and orange juice. Even the coffee was fresh. He had an arrangement with the concierge to stock his refrigerator when he made his brief forays to town.

Once he'd thought of the condo as the ultimate bachelor pad, perfect for entertaining, for bringing girlfriends. Simple to lock it and leave if he decided to go somewhere else for a few weeks, as he so often did. He'd always been restless.

He'd never brought Fanny here, of course. Very few people knew about Fanny. His mother, the Klassens, his lawyer and best friend, Scott Carradine—all people he could trust.

And now Eva Haines.

Did he trust her? Whether he did or not, there was nothing he could do about her friendship with his daughter. She didn't know anything about Fanny except that she was a sweet little girl with a big dog and a lot of curiosity. Plus, Eva would be leaving the island soon. Going back to her own life. He had to keep his mind fixed on that.

Eva Haines had turned out to be more of a risk to his peace of mind than he'd thought possible. He couldn't stop thinking about her, which was half the reason he'd decided to come to Vancouver for a few days. Okay, *most* of the reason.

There was another reason. He checked his watch and reached for the phone. Still too early to call Fanny. He punched in a series of numbers. Scott would be up. You didn't make partner in one of

Vancouver's most prestigious law firms at thirty-four by sleeping past seven. He badly needed to talk to him.

SILAS USED HIS KEY to enter the premises of his shop, Silas Lord Creations, on the fourth floor of the art deco Steingart Building on Thurlow Street, just off Robson. The doors were kept locked as a security measure. Silas Lord Creations had a lot of valuable inventory on the premises. His customers didn't walk in off the street; they made appointments.

"Anything happening, Tracy?"

"Silas!" Tracy Figueira, his personal assistant and manager of the small showroom, glanced up in surprise. "I wasn't expecting you."

"When are you ever expecting me?" he teased. Tracy was a treasure. She not only looked after the showroom and answered questions from potential customers, she also acted as secretary for his various other business ventures, most notably a one-third share in the West Vancouver marina run by his uncle Leo. His father, Leo's twin brother, Arden, had taken a late midlife crisis very seriously and divested himself of all his family responsibilities six years ago—including Silas's mother. He'd moved to an island off the New Zealand coast, where he lived in a beachfront house with a series of much younger partners. Fanny, Silas often mused, came by her party-animal genes honestly on both sides.

Tracy reached into a desk drawer and handed him a sheaf of unopened mail. ''Here. Most of this was personal or gallery stuff or stuff I didn't know what to do with so I saved it for you.''

''Aren't you kind?'' He hated dealing with correspondence. He'd had to train himself to pay more attention to details like that since he'd become involved with his uncle's business. Uncle Leo was very exacting about particulars. Silas would rather have been in his studio, casting metal or dreaming up new designs. He turned over the envelope on top and ripped it open. From the Casman-Spencer Gallery on South Granville. An invitation to a launch by some up-and-coming sculptor that very evening. The timing was lucky. He'd go. He needed a diversion, plus Scott would likely be there.

''Anything sell since I was in last?''

Silas sauntered into the small showroom, each item in its own brightly lit secure display case. He especially wanted to see the neckpiece he'd done a few months back for a client who'd changed her mind. Red amber and hammered silver. He'd ended up doing something else for her, a twisted gold bracelet with opals. He hadn't felt right about the amber piece, anyway; women often suited one type of jewelry or another, and the client was definitely an opal type.

''The jade necklace and earrings sold last week.''

"Oh?"

"A customer from Japan. Money no object. He and his wife were very interested in the onyx bracelets, too. We might hear from them again. I also sold the anklet."

"Who bought that?" Silas smiled. He'd made the silver ankle cuff for fun, quite certain it would never sell. He'd been wrong, obviously.

"A dancer, oddly enough."

Silas frowned. *Vivian.* He'd been attracted to her as a dancer before he'd ever thought of asking her to model. "Dancer?"

"Yes. A principal with the Winnipeg Ballet. She thought it was charming."

Ah. *That* kind of dancer. Silas smiled, glad the cuff had found a home, his mind already playing with the image of a prima ballerina *en pointe* with the cuff gleaming under the lights.

"Listen, Tracy, can you get the Chiapas piece out for me? I want to take it back to the island. I have an idea for some changes I'd like to make." His office manager produced her key and removed the silver neckpiece, glowing with the precious so-called red amber, really more a deep wine color, from Mexico's southernmost province. Silas preferred Mexican amber to Baltic. He prized the brilliance, the range of color.

Tracy handed it to him. "It's beautiful just as it is Silas. Don't change it too much."

The necklace burned in his pocket all day while he ran various other errands. He knew why he'd taken it and yet he wished he hadn't acted on the impulse. He'd dreamed of Eva wearing this ever since he'd discovered her at The Baths. *Seawater and kelp, silver and amber.* It was an indulgence, a foolish whim, to take the piece away with him to Liberty Island.

Of course, he'd never see her wearing it.

SILAS HAD SUPPER delivered from a deli on Denman Street and ate while rapidly going through the statements his Uncle Leo had left for him. Now that Arden Lord had withdrawn from the business—"gone to bush," Leo said—it was mainly Silas and his uncle in charge. Leo, who ran the West Vancouver marina, had never married and Silas was an only child. Silas had one aunt, a considerably younger half sister to the twins, but she lived in Montreal and had never taken an active role in the family businesses.

At nine he had a shower, shaved, pulled on a linen jacket over a clean black T-shirt and jeans and called a cab. As he waited for the elevator, he glanced in the mirrors that lined the hall and ran one hand over his shaggy, sun-bleached locks. Damn! Definitely should have gotten a haircut. By the time he'd gone through the list Tracy had lined up for him, the day was over. Maybe tomorrow. He planned to have lunch with his mother and then spend a few hours in the afternoon in his workshop adjacent to the showroom. Then some shopping, a gift for Fanny, perhaps a sun hat since she was so taken with the one Eva always wore and, next day, he'd fly home. He might even call someone Saturday, actually go out on a date.

The Casman-Spencer Gallery on South Granville Street was part of a brightly lit strip between Tenth and Eleventh Avenues. He spotted Scott a few minutes after he arrived. Plenty of beautiful people, allowing for the time of year. Summer wasn't the favored season for gallery openings but this one was packed. Tall women, good teeth, wafts of expensive perfume, waiters pushing through the crowds bearing aloft trays of hors d'oeuvres and cocktails. The C and S, as it was known, was famous for its rambunctious events and Silas hoped tonight's would be no exception. He scored a glass of champagne from a passing waiter and drank it down. He needed to get some perspective on the feelings he'd been trying to bury all week. Home, family, permanence, security. Safety. *Love.* He returned the glass to the silver tray and reached for another.

Islands were strange places. It was easy to get your priorities mixed up.

"Hey!" Scott appeared in front of him with two women, one on each arm. Both tall, both with ample breasts and both quite familiar-looking. Silas had a sinking feeling that he might have slept with one of them before, but damned if he could think of their names. There were several women in the room, actually, who fit that particular bill.

"Hey," Silas said with a grin. Good old Scott. He never changed.

He suffered Scott's awkward one-armed hug and then, before he realized what was happening, the two blondes had their faces pressed against his and a flashbulb went off. The women laughed and one—Trish?—pulled out a tissue to wipe lipstick from his face.

Silas grinned, trying to be a good sport about whatever was going on. "It's not my birthday, ladies."

Scott roared. "Welcome back to the city, pal!"

The camera, of course, belonged to Zack Sperry, the *Vancouver Sun*'s ubiquitous in-your-face social columnist. Didn't he ever take time off? Silas supposed not, with free drinks and sushi on offer somewhere in the city every evening of the week. Many times in the past, Silas had opened the paper to see his mug in Sperry's column after a night on the town. It was getting old. Surely Silas Lord, whose partying days were long over, was yesterday's news. The gadfly ought to chase fresh material.

Scott grabbed a cocktail from a passing tray and put his arm around Silas's neck again. Ignored, the two women melted into the noisy crowd. "Okay, so what's with all this talk about taking some action to settle things all of a sudden? I know, I know, it's been three years. I'm doing what I can. We need to find Vivian first."

Silas nodded. Vivian was the key to the problem, all right.

He leaned closer and Silas could tell that Scott hadn't had as much to drink as he'd thought at first. "Listen up—and this is a respected member of the bar, your Uncle Scottie talkin', in case you've forgotten. You need to lie low, just keep doing what you're doing. You don't need any more complications in your life. Settling down. Getting domestic. What the *hell?* You're crazy even to think like that!"

He looked behind them, as though they might be overheard, which was highly unlikely in the din. "You've got too much going on. Give me time, I'm *on* it—"

Silas shrugged. How could he explain to Scott the way he'd been thinking? Feeling? *Hoping?* Scott was his best friend. They went way back, before

Ivor had been hurt. Scott had been there—Silas hadn't—at Garden Bay when it happened, one of a group of six boys jumping off rocks into the bay. Yet Scott never enquired about Ivor, never mentioned the subject.

He didn't understand what Silas wanted, that Silas needed something more in his life. That something had to *happen.* How could he—Silas—go forward when so much of the past was still tying him up? He'd been frozen, in a state of self-inflicted paralysis, for nearly three years. Sure, Scott was trying to resolve the situation, but when was Silas going to see results?

Maybe they'd been pals all their lives, but at this moment, he and Scott were inhabiting two different planets, standing right there in the same room, drinking the same free champagne, eating the same designer munchies. Scott was a high flyer, enjoying the good life, just as Silas had done once. Silas was the one who'd changed. He was a father, now, and a serious craftsman, plying both arts in the solitude of Liberty Island. A place that didn't even have electricity or proper running water, for crying out loud.

Silas put his glass down, still half-full. The champagne tasted sour. No, Liberty Island was a long way from being perfect. But it was what he had right now.

"Where you off to, buddy?" Scott's expression was incredulous when he realized Silas's intent.

"It's been a long day. I'll give you a call in the morning."

"No way! Trish here—*hey,* where'd she go?" The lawyer stretched his neck, searching over the heads of the crowd. "She says she knows you from a while back. We got lots of stuff planned for the evening." He winked at Silas. "Come on, the night's just starting. I thought you came to town for some fun?"

Silas repeated his apologies and headed for the door. Scott's point was valid. Yes, why *had* he suddenly decided to come to town? The night before, he'd walked Eva home and then spent the entire next day thinking about her. He'd thrown his tools down in disgust midafternoon and gone for a sail by himself in the strait.

He'd come to town for *exactly* this—to meet some people, do some business, talk to friends, maybe even get laid.

Forget about Eva. Scott was right. He didn't need the complications. She might not see the situation his way. She might even go to the police.

He shouldered his way toward the street, nodded to several people he knew, said hello to a few others. On the sidewalk at last, he took a deep breath of the still-hot, exhaust-scented night air and started walking north, toward the Granville Bridge. It would take him a least forty-five minutes to reach the condo, maybe more, but the walk was what he wanted.

The trip hadn't been worthless. He knew something now that he hadn't known last night, or this morning. He might be mixed up about a lot of things but he was crystal-clear on one: he definitely didn't want any more Trishs in his life.

CHAPTER TWELVE

THE PIPER CUB had to fight the rising wind the last few nautical miles as Silas flew to the small bay just off The Baths where he generally brought down the floatplane. From there, he'd motor to the wharf in front of the house where he could tie up securely.

So much for the weather change forecast for tomorrow, he thought grimly, bringing the little craft into a tight turn to approach the landing upwind. He was glad he'd decided to come back early. It was a disappointment for his mother, who almost never came to Liberty Island, the scene of many unhappy memories for her, but who loved to see whatever new photos he had of Fanny, her only grandchild. Greta Lord had never become a Canadian citizen. She still traveled on a Swedish passport and in the back of his mind, Silas sometimes entertained the idea of going to his mother's birthplace and starting over. With Fanny, of course. And the tools of his trade. His craft and his reputation were portable.

"Go to bush" just like his father, Silas's Uncle

Leo would probably say. ''There's Lords and there's scoundrels,'' his uncle would remark dryly. ''We got plenty of both in this family.''

Was escaping to Sweden a coward's way out? Maybe. It hadn't come to that yet but Silas couldn't rule out any options. One thing he did know—he would never be parted from Fanny.

Silas had had his pilot's license for over ten years and he'd made far more difficult landings. He secured the aircraft, double-checked the moorings on the boats because of the oncoming storm, although he knew Matthew would have done the job properly, then ran up the steps to the graveled path that led to the house, his satchel over his shoulder and his head down. The wind was gusting furiously already, with dark clouds rolling in from the northwest.

A welcome summer storm, long overdue. Take the dust off the trees and the tension out of the air. There'd be a couple of hours' downpour and then sunshine again.

Silas burst into the house via the kitchen door, stamping the first licks of rain from his sandals. ''Fanny?'' he called.

''Shhh!'' Aggie appeared in the hallway. ''She's having a little lie-down. Poor mite is worn-out.''

Silas frowned. ''Why?'' His daughter was usually a dynamo of energy. ''She sick?''

''Too much excitement these days, that's all.

She's been playing dress-up all day with the clothes and stuff Eva sent over and she sat right here all afternoon and made a whole bunch of new invitations."

Silas grinned and slung his leather satchel off his shoulder onto the table. "Damn—another party?"

"Yes. And you'd better be willing to attend, too," the housekeeper said severely. "She wants me to make cupcakes. Any sign of Matthew?"

"No. Where is he?"

"I'm worried. He said he was going to take down that old Anjou tree and chop it up for firewood. He got his chain saw and the wheelbarrow two or three hours ago. I don't like him out there with a storm coming on."

Silas held up his hand. "I'll go find him, Aggie. You take this and put it at the end of Fanny's bed." He handed her the sun hat, which he'd had gift-wrapped at the shop on Burrard Street. "She'll find it when she wakes up."

He dug in his bag again. "And *this* is for you." He handed her a box of Purdy's chocolates, tied with a purple bow. Miniatures. They were Aggie's favorite, although, considering the number she usually ate at one sitting, jumbos would have made more sense and she could have comforted herself that she'd had "just a few."

"Oh, Silas!" Aggie's cheeks were pink. "You're such a thoughtful man! And so *kind* to us."

"Don't say it!" Silas wrapped his arms around the housekeeper's dumpling of a body and gave her a fierce hug. "I couldn't manage without the two of you, you know that. I could never repay you and Matthew for what you've done for me and Fanny."

"Oh, Silas—"

Silas put his finger over her mouth. "Not another word." He exchanged his sandals for some sneakers that were by the door and went out again. The wind nearly took away his breath. It was getting darker, too, although it wasn't much past five o'clock. Aggie was right; Matthew should've come in by now.

Eva. How was she doing in that dilapidated house in a wind like this? He hoped the roof wouldn't blow off. Damn. He'd promised himself he wasn't going to think about her....

"Matthew!" Silas could see the downed pear tree on the far side of the orchard, but there was no sign of the old man. Alarmed, he broke into a run. "Matthew!"

He spotted a movement by the thick barrier of gorse and broom that separated the far end of the orchard from the shore, protecting the trees from the wind and weather off the open water. Matthew emerged from the thicket, adjusting his overalls.

He'd obviously just walked into the bushes to relieve himself. Still, Aggie was right. Time for him to come in. She'd have dinner on the table soon.

"Hey!"

Matthew waved in response to Silas's shout and Silas slowed to a walk. No sense scaring the old guy. He was always working at something. That was Matthew. When he sat down, he was as still as stone. Never read, rarely watched television. Weeding the garden, bringing in firewood, fixing a fence—Matthew liked staying busy. Silas often felt guilty that the Klassens still worked for him, as they'd done for his parents, taking care of the Lord estate on Liberty Island when they'd already retired once to their cottage by the sea near Ivor. Another reason Silas needed to resolve his situation—and quickly.

On the other hand, wouldn't Matthew run out of things to do with nothing but a bit of lawn to mow and a few rows of lettuce to tend?

"Just about time to eat," Silas said as Matthew approached. "Here, I'll give you a hand. We'll take one load and come back for the rest tomorrow." Silas began heaving chunks of wood into the wheelbarrow.

As he'd expected, dinner was on the table when they returned to the house. Fanny was up, her new sun hat on her head, and the instant she saw him, she launched herself into his arms. "Daddy! Thank you for the nice hat. It's just like Eva's!"

"Only smaller."

"Right. Only smaller." Silas bent down and tied the dangling strings. Fanny wasn't that adept yet at tying her shoes, so he imagined the strings under her chin would give her trouble. "I guess you're going to have to learn how to tie these so it'll stay on."

"I tried, Daddy, but I got all insided out."

"I think you mean 'mixed up,' don't you?"

"No," she said mischievously, untying the bow he'd made, and taking off the hat again. "Insided out!"

Mashed potatoes, beef stew, fresh peas from the garden. Silas liked these family dinners. They reminded him of his own childhood summers on Liberty Island. They'd even had the same cook and gardener, although much younger versions then, and in those days, Ivor would've been sitting with them, trying some new magic or card trick he'd learned. "So, anything exciting happen while I was away?"

"Ha!" Mrs. Klassen scoffed. "You know nothing ever happens here—now, that's not true," she corrected herself. "I ran into Eva shopping at the Bluebird Bakery in Gibsons on Friday. Isn't that a coincidence?"

"I suppose it is," he said tersely. He didn't want

to talk about Eva Haines. *So, she'd gone to the mainland again….*

"She was running errands, I think, in an old red truck. She carried Ivor's cheesecake out to the car for me. I expect she probably stopped in to see—ah…" Aggie paused and gave him a self-conscious look. Until Eva Haines's arrival, they'd never spoken about the other end of the island or the woman who lived there. "You know, the old lady at the, ah, lodge where she lives now. In Sechelt, I believe."

"I got some of the old lady's jewels," Fanny chimed in. "That's Eva's cousin, Daddy. Eva gived them to me."

"*Gave,* honey," Silas said automatically, "not *gived.*" He made a mental note to check the so-called "jewels" his daughter had brought home. Silas had never been told what was behind the Lord-Bonhomme family feud—if, indeed, his father or uncle or mother actually knew—but he wouldn't risk adding heat to the flames by letting his daughter inadvertently accept any possibly valuable Bonhomme trinket. Whatever the feud was, it meant nothing to him. There was only one person alive who cared—the old woman in the nursing home. Tiresome as it was, Silas had respected Doris Bonhomme's desire to be ignored. Indeed, he'd gone farther. He'd cooperated so far as to maintain the fiction that he wasn't aware she existed. As for the Klassens, they were used to the foolishness; they'd been part of it since they'd begun working on the island thirty years before.

"Gave, gave, gave," his daughter repeated in a low singsong, making a volcano out of her small puddle of potatoes and gravy.

"I didn't see her boat tied up this morning," Matthew volunteered unexpectedly. "I might take a walk over there after dinner and see if she's come back."

"She wouldn't cross the strait in this weather!" Silas looked sharply at the caretaker. As though to underline his concern, an unsecured shutter crashed against a window. "She may have gone fishing or something this morning."

"Nope." The old man shook his head. "Boat wasn't there last evening, neither."

"She must've stayed overnight on the mainland," Aggie interjected. "Perhaps tonight, too. I'm sure she has friends there, a lovely young woman like that. Or perhaps she's gone to Vancouver to visit her father." She looked from her husband to Silas and back again, then finished stoutly, "She doesn't need to keep *us* informed."

Silas tried to hide his alarm. "I hear a couple of shutters banging." He pushed back from the table.

"Thank you for the meal, Aggie. Maybe you can help me with the windows, Matthew."

Silas supervised Fanny's bath and then played two games of Snakes and Ladders with the girl at the kitchen table. He heard every gust of wind and felt every lash of rain as though he was out in the weather himself. He couldn't concentrate on the game, which wasn't a huge problem. Fanny was delighted to win and then she insisted he read her favorite Curious George story—twice. Finally, nine o'clock rolled around and he tucked her into bed.

"Sweet dreams, baby," he said, kissing her cheek.

"Sweet dreams, Daddy," she said, her eyes shining. "I sure like that new hat you brought me. I'm gonna surprise Eva when I wear it tomorrow."

He carried out the lamp. Fanny's window was bare to starlight and moonlight, most nights. Tonight, due to the storm, Silas closed the curtains. The entire house was fitted out with old-fashioned gas lights, mostly kerosene. Some were Aladdin lamps, which had tall slender chimneys and gave off considerable illumination. When Silas had first returned to the island to live, he'd been frustrated with the various finicky lighting contraptions, but now he was used to the soft glow and mellow shadows.

Silas had told Matthew he'd check on Eva himself. With Fanny in bed, he could finally take some action on what had been on his mind all evening—Eva's boat.

If it was tied up and secure at the Bonhomme wharf, that would mean she was all right, too.

CHAPTER THIRTEEN

SILAS STOPPED to wipe his eyes, cursing as a rain-laden cedar branch smacked across his face. The wind had shifted slightly to the north and blew steadily with gusts that whipped trees into a frenzy and sent wet branches slamming furiously this way and that. He couldn't see a thing beyond the thin arc of his flashlight, except for the water running along the gutter in the rocks before him on the path and the branches looming suddenly, reaching for him from the darkness on either side of the trail. The moon, nearly full tonight, was completely obscured by storm clouds.

He pushed on. The journey to the split in the path was less than a third of a mile, a ten-minute walk, yet tonight it seemed endless. He watched carefully for the faint track that bore to the left, toward the creek crossing and the Bonhomme house. There'd been very little traffic along that trail over the years. Now, with everything wet, it was even harder to see. If he went too far, he'd end up at The Baths. The flashlight beam revealed only crude light and shadow, black and white.

Still, he knew the way.

Silas found the fork, and noticed a bedraggled loop of yarn still hanging from a broken branch about four feet from the ground. Fanny-height. Part of the "map" she'd made so Eva could find her way to the party. Clever girl. Had it really only been last Tuesday? Five short days ago?

He emerged from the trees into the full force of the gale. He'd been protected, to some degree, in the forest. What was that sound, though, beneath the howl of the wind? The creek? It had risen several inches and frothed with foam and muddy water, spilling over the rocks and the slippery fallen tree normally used to cross the stream. Silas made his way gingerly through the water, feeling for sound footing in the rough creek bed as he went. The water surged past his knees. His shirt was soaked, and now his jeans were wet, too.

He was probably crazy—he *knew* he was crazy! This was worse than those times he'd felt compelled to creep through the forest to spy on the old woman, make sure she had enough firewood, see that the runabout, her only way off the island, was secure. Chances were, Eva was sound asleep, safe in bed, her boat safe, too. Even the damn donkey was probably snoring in the woodshed, waiting out the storm.

The only one stupid enough to venture out in weather like this was Silas.

But he knew he couldn't have stayed home. He wouldn't have slept, not knowing....

There was no light in the house but that didn't mean anything. On Liberty Island, lamps were only used when necessary. Why waste kerosene to light up the whole house if you were reading in bed?

Out in the open, Silas could see a little more. There was a glow from the water, perhaps a reflection of some distant, angled moonlight. The storm hadn't let up yet, but it would soon either blow itself out or move on.

He walked in the direction of her wharf, past the boulder—Big Rock, it had always been called—that edged the shore to the west of Doris Bonhomme's small harbor. What was that? Pebbles rattling? The scrape of a hoof? Perhaps the donkey *was* roaming about....

"Andy!" he shouted, but there was no answering hee-haw, no goofy splay-eared donkey's head looming out of the shadows. Silas continued on.

The dock was a disgrace. Pilings leaning, planks in the platform itself warped and cracked, chains rusted. What did he expect? The old woman had been too damn stubborn to leave, but she'd been in no condition to live here by herself. The proof was everywhere, from the broken-down fence he'd jumped over—through was more like it—the first time he'd come looking for Fanny, a fence that kept nothing in *or* out of her garden—to the missing shingles on the roof, and the dock, before him now, heaving and creaking on the turbulent water, ready to float away with the next combination of a high winter tide and another storm like this.

Silas ventured out onto the unsteady wharf. *The boat was there.*

He didn't realize how worried he'd been until he saw the ghostly outline of the runabout, bucking against the pressure of its well-tied lines, gunwales squealing where they made contact with the splintered timbers of the wharf. He stared, shocked, suddenly aware of how hard his heart was pounding, how much his lungs hurt.

This wasn't about making sure his temporary neighbor—Doris's cousin—was okay. That her boat was tied down, that her roof hadn't blown off…

This was about something much bigger.

EVA BEGAN battening down the hatches on the old house about suppertime, when the wind started to rise. When she'd returned from Half Moon Bay just after noon, she'd taken a long walk around the western end of the island, tracing the southern shore to the outcropping at the western tip, where she'd sat for a few hours, enjoying the sunshine and watching sea lions play on the distant rocks between Liberty and Monterrey Island. Beyond that lay Lasqueti and, to the north, Hornby and Quadra, and beyond those large islands lay the massive outline of Vancouver Island. At night, from this vantage point, you could see the lights of Nanaimo.

She'd seen the harbingers of the storm, the cloud build-up and the massive ledge that indicated two fronts colliding. The sailing and power squadron courses she'd taken at her father's insistence as a teenager hadn't been entirely wasted. She wasn't sure how much navigation she remembered, but she hadn't forgotten weather signs. The poplars and trembling aspens had that silvery, fluttery look that preceded rain.

She returned to the house via the north shore, clambering over a rock-strewn route she rarely took. She hadn't slept well the night before. The fresh air and vigorous exercise would do her good.

Eva hadn't seen anyone from the other side of the island, which was a relief. She adored the little girl, but it was just as well not to get too attached to her in the short time remaining. Eva had made up her mind to concentrate on her duties and stop obsessing about her neighbor. Get the job done and move on. No matter what his circumstances—and there were plenty of men who weren't married to or living with the mothers of their children—he deserved a summer free of her nosy questions and imaginings. He was clearly a private sort. An artist. What right did she have to interfere with a man's desire for peace and privacy? She'd see Fanny occasionally and she'd invite Mrs. Klassen over for tea or lunch one or two afternoons, avoid The Baths, and generally keep to herself until it was time to leave.

There were several more boatloads of goods to transfer to the mainland, she couldn't take too many at once without swamping the runabout. But other than that, and finding a place for Andy, Eva didn't intend to go anywhere until she was finished with her responsibilities here. She still needed to discuss the details of Doris's plan with someone at the Gulf Islands Marine Trust in Vancouver, but perhaps she could arrange that later, after she'd left the island, and there'd be no need to come back again.

She'd allowed herself to get carried away with the mystery that surrounded the old feud between her second cousin and the Lord family. She'd been swept up by romantic notions of piracy and glamour, centered now, she realized, on the handsome, enigmatic Silas Lord, the current occupant and owner of the eastern half of the island. These ideas dated from the childhood games she and her sisters had played during blissful summers on Liberty Island, much as Fanny Lord held "parties" for squirrels and dogs today. They were pure imagination.

She needed to be realistic and practical, as she'd always been. She needed to look toward the future, the *real* future. A contract for the fall, teaching full-time. If a job offer came from the Interior or Vancouver Island, she'd need to think about moving, about subletting her small apartment in Burnaby....

After a cold meal—avocado and tuna salad on Bluebird Bakery rye bread—Eva went out to the shed for some extra firewood. The air still held its summer heat but the storm was fast approaching across the strait and the wind was gusting furiously. The house was relatively comfortable now but a storm could change everything. The old house was like a colander. Weather stripping had not been a concept in Doris's world. Even the windows were ancient, bubbled single-pane glass, many of them cracked. The shutters afforded some protection, she supposed, but it must have been chilly in the winters. No wonder her cousin had traveled so much, at least in her younger days.

Andy stayed close to her, getting in the way and looking mournful as she secured a few shutters and put away the wheelbarrow. Eva enticed him into the woodshed with a handful of oats and put him in the roomy box stall that formed one half of the small structure. He brayed his displeasure at being shut in and bobbed his head vigorously but Eva ignored him. He'd stay warm and dry in here and she'd let him out in the morning. The other side of the shed was littered with a dwindling wood supply. There was no need to worry about getting more. Doris would never be returning and, in a week or so, Eva would be gone, too.

A sad thought.

Eva lit several lamps, glad she'd laid in plenty of wicks and oil and spare candles, and read for a while in the flickering light at the kitchen table. The storm blew fiercely, and somewhere upstairs, a shutter banged, or perhaps it was a branch from one of the trees growing too near the house. For the first time she really did feel a bit spooked, being alone here.

She decided to play the piano for a while, just for the company, and set an Aladdin lamp on top of the instrument so she could see the notes on some of Doris's old sheet music, whatever had escaped the thrift store boxes so far. She gave up after twenty minutes. The sticking E and F keys were a nuisance and the piano was so out of tune it was annoying. And, somehow, the pool of light around it only emphasized the darkness in the rest of the room.

Eva checked the clock in the kitchen. Half-past eight, but dark as midnight outside with the wind howling around the corners of the house and the rain hammering against the glass. She blew out the lamps and took one with her up the stairs to her bedroom under the eaves. Perhaps she'd read for a while. Tonight she'd definitely find out if the roof leaked; this storm would be a good test.

EVA MUST HAVE fallen asleep with the lamp on. She awoke to the acrid smell of smouldering kerosene and the sound of hammering somewhere in the house. At first, startled and still half-asleep, she thought it was a shutter banging but she soon realized someone was knocking on the kitchen door downstairs.

She heard a shout.

Frightened, Eva put on her robe and fastened it around her waist. She grabbed the sputtering lamp in shaky fingers and crept down the stairs, taking care not to stumble.

She set the lamp on the table. Who could it be? It must be someone from the other side of the island—

"Silas!"

The door practically blew open as soon as she unlatched it and he stood there, leaning against the doorjamb, soaked from head to toe. He was breathing heavily and he had a strange look in his eyes.

"What is it? What's wrong?" Fear gripped her heart. "Has something happened to—"

"No," he replied, breathing heavily. Had he been

running? ‘‘Fanny, Matthew, Aggie—everyone’s okay.’’

She opened the door a little wider but he made no move to come in. His eyes held hers. She was glad she’d put the lamp down or she knew she’d have dropped it—sent the whole place up in flames.

‘‘How about you? Are *you* all right?’’

Eva tried to smile but her face felt dry, tight. Frozen. ‘‘I—I’m fine. Terrible storm, isn’t it?’’

‘‘Yes,’’ he said, still with that strange look. ‘‘It is. Terrible.’’

Then he pulled her into his arms.

CHAPTER FOURTEEN

EVA RECOILED as the icy chill of Silas's body penetrated the thin cotton of her wrap. She flung up one hand, thinking to ward him off, but, instead, her arm slid around his neck as he hauled her against him, one arm around her waist, the other gripping her shoulders tightly, fingers splayed. He forced her face to meet the angle of his. His mouth was anything but cold.

Eva kissed him back, her soul rallying, the rest of her in shock. She clung to him, aware of the rain on his face, his hair. He even *smelled* of the wind. He shifted his stance, held her even more tightly, kissed her more deeply....

This was the stuff of dreams—perhaps she *was* dreaming. Perhaps she'd fallen asleep and her restless mind had conjured up the swashbuckler of her girlish imaginings, the pirate returned from the sea to carry off the woman he loved....

"Silas!" She fought to make sense of it as he kissed her face, her nose, her eyes, her forehead, as he muttered her name over and over.

"Shut up," he whispered and covered her mouth with his again.

All the blood in her body rushed to the surface, bringing with it unbearable heat. How much was simple reaction to the unexpected chill of the wind at the open door? How much a response to his kisses?

The brief flash of lightning followed by immediate thunder overhead did nothing to return Eva to her senses. But the sound, a few seconds later, of a crash somewhere in the house and the tinkling of glass did.

Silas stared into her eyes. She felt consumed by the fire she saw there. Was it the reflection from the lamp? "What the hell was that?"

"I—I don't know," she whispered, then the lamp she'd left on the table went out.

Silas strode into the kitchen and Eva reached for the door, pushing it closed against the fury of the storm and latching it. She felt along the shelf next to the doorframe. Ah! Matches and the candles. Her hands shook so much she could barely strike the match.

"Damn!" She heard Silas bang into something, probably a chair.

"Hold on, I've got a light," she called, the linoleum cool under her bare feet as she edged along, feeling her way. She was freezing, trembling violently, and she couldn't figure out why. Then she realized the entire front of her robe was damp from Silas's wet clothing.

"Over here." Silas stood in the next room, where the piano was, near the window.

Eva raised the candle and it promptly went out but before it did, she glimpsed the broken branch thrusting through the lower panes of the French doors.

"Stand back," Silas ordered. Eva had seen the shards and splinters all over the floor and she froze, afraid to step forward or back.

Silas moved toward her and she felt his hands on her arms. Then he cursed again and she gasped as he lifted her bodily and carried her into the kitchen and set her down.

"Do you think you could relight that oil lamp on the table?" he asked in a surprisingly calm voice. "It might be better than the candle."

Eva felt along the shelf again for the box of matches, then fumbled with the lamp, removing the chimney and holding a light to the untrimmed wick. It smoked and flared unevenly and she replaced the chimney with both hands. Then she slowly raised her eyes to meet Silas's gaze across the table.

The raw hunger in his expression made her pulse jump but she noticed that his voice was steady when he spoke. "Maybe you could hold it in the doorway of the other room.'' He turned. ''Don't go in or you'll cut your feet. I'll put something across that window.''

Eva held the lantern high while Silas pushed a large wooden cabinet, one Eva hadn't gone through yet, across the room. He forced the tree limb back outside, through the broken pane, then positioned the dresser so it covered the gaping hole. Eva noticed the difference in the room immediately. No wind. Quiet.

''You look like the Statue of Liberty,'' he said wryly, coming to stand in front of her. Eva managed a tremulous smile and lowered the lamp.

''I'm sorry,'' he said quickly, then took the lamp from her hand and traced her lips with his thumb. ''There's nothing humorous about this, is there?'' She took a deep breath, pure reaction, and closed her eyes.

''Eva.'' His voice was ragged and she noticed that the shadows from the lamp danced on the ceiling. ''Eva, I've wanted you from the first moment I saw you. At The Baths. You were the most glorious, most beautiful woman I'd ever seen and I couldn't believe it when I found your name was so close to Eve. The first woman…''

Eva was dazzled by his words. ''What are you talking about?'' she whispered. She opened her eyes and stared into his. The wavering flame from the lamp he held was reflected there. *As was she.*

"You know what I'm talking about." He leaned forward and hesitated, his mouth inches away. Eva saw his mouth so near, his lips, the rough stubble on his chin, the dark planes of his face, the haunted question in his eyes. Then she placed her mouth on his. They kissed softly at first, tenderly, until Eva grew bolder and moved closer, pressing her body against his.

He took a step toward the table, to set down the lamp, then he reached for her and kissed her again and again. At last, when she thought she might faint, he swung her into his arms, turning sideways as he bore her up the narrow stairs. At the top, he paused. "Which way?" His voice was harsh.

"Left," she replied, knowing exactly what he meant. What he intended. What *she* intended…

He shouldered open the door to her room, ducking to avoid bumping his head on the low ceiling, and deposited her on the narrow bed.

Eva could barely see him in the dark, with only the low glow of light from the water coming through the window. There were candles on the table beside the bed but she didn't bother to light one now. He stripped off his shirt, over his head, and she unbelted her robe. She wore nothing underneath. He leaned down and pulled the fabric aside, gazing at her for one long moment that turned Eva's skin to cinders. Then he lowered himself onto the narrow bed beside her.

Eva turned eagerly into his arms, the heat and hard length of his body so welcome against hers. She raised her face, met his mouth yet again, and felt joy seep through every pore....

She was not dreaming now.

Silas Lord, the man who'd filled her dreams so often since she'd arrived on Liberty Island, was here beside her. In her bed. In her arms.

In her heart.

A CLEAN COOL night breeze, smelling of summer, was blowing through the partially opened window when Eva awoke. She heard the occasional *whoosh* of raindrops on the roof as the big cedars and arbutus trees growing near the house responded to the occasional billow of wind passing over the island, tatters of the storm that had moved on. Perhaps that was the sound that had disturbed her.

It wasn't dawn yet—she had no idea what time it was—but she could see clearly beyond the rectangle of the bare window. If she sat up in bed, she knew she'd be able to make out the shore, the wharf with the *Edie B.* tied up and the distant outlines of other islands slumbering in the strait.

The moonlight cast a glow on the naked outline

of Silas's body next to hers. She was squeezed between him and the wall but she wasn't complaining. Two in a small bed made for plenty of heat, in more ways than one, and either she or Silas had thrown off the quilt at some point. Eva reached for the rumpled sheet at her knees, and covered them both lightly to the waist. She buried her elbow in the pillow and gazed down at the man beside her.

How could she, who had led such a calm, uneventful, *ordinary* life, have come to this? She'd had lovers, had even been engaged once. Briefly. She couldn't quite remember what had gone wrong there, which was a comment on the relationship, she supposed. She'd never had her heart broken. She wasn't sure she believed all that romantic nonsense about hearts breaking. That was for country-and-western crooners. Or for Kate, her sister who'd gone off to Africa to slay dragons. Or for the movies. Not for quiet, sensible Eva Haines.

And yet…

Eva pushed her hair behind her ear as it fell in front of her face. *This man could break her heart.* She felt she was on some precipice. Some place in her life where she had to make a commitment. Take a chance. She'd thought it was about getting a new job, but maybe that wasn't it at all. Maybe Liberty Island, the last place she'd have expected, held the key to her life. Her future.

A shiver rippled over her bare skin, the rain whooshed again on the roof and Eva glanced up at the ceiling, to see if there were any widening stains, any drips coming down into the tiny bedroom. She expected there would be, considering the number of shingles that were curled up and useless or missing. She wiggled her toes. The bed, so far as she could tell, wasn't soggy anywhere.

When she glanced back, Silas was awake. His eyes were open, watchful, and he smiled, ever so slightly as her gaze froze on his. She smiled, too, catching her breath. Feeling the tiniest quiver of fear. What now? She wasn't good at mornings-after; she hadn't had a lot of them.

One night of passion, she knew, meant very little in the scheme of things. Besides his asking, at some crucial point, if she was protected, they hadn't spoken.

"You're awake?" His voice was sleepy and thick.

"I was looking for leaks in the ceiling," she admitted, "but I couldn't find any." He reached up and ran his fingers through her hair, which had escaped again and hung like a dark wing before her eyes.

"So practical." He smiled. "And so beautiful," he added, in a wondering voice. It embarrassed Eva; no one had ever called her *beautiful* before.

Her instinct was denial. "I'm not, Silas."

"You are," he said, his finger closing her mouth. "You're so beautiful to me I—I cannot describe it. I cannot understand it." His eyes held hers, as uncertain, in a way, as she felt. "I accept it, though," he finished. "It's a *gift.*"

She took a long, slow breath. "Beauty?" She tried for a laugh, which never emerged. "What *is* that?"

"Beauty is a mystery, I agree. But it's also truth, the truth I trust. You are the most beautiful woman I have ever met, Eva. Do you believe me?"

Eva stared at him. Was he joking with her? "You've probably said that to many women."

"I've never said it to *any* woman," he said in a rough voice, pulling her to him and kissing her. "Only you," he whispered as he released her.

Eva had to believe him. He wrapped his arms around her and when she raised her face to his, she was surprised that his kiss this time was gentle. Almost chaste. She bent her head and drew in the scent of his skin. Sea kelp, storm water and—mud?

She listened to the deep, steady thunder of his pulse, felt it quicken slightly. "There's something I have to tell you, Eva." His voice echoed, tangled with the rhythm of his heart. She felt him tense. "I need to be honest with you. I don't expect you to support me, but I want you to listen to what I have to say. Everything I'm going to tell you is the absolute truth.''

What could it be? He wasn't married. He had no wife. Surely that was the only truth that mattered, considering their intimate circumstances here in her narrow bed in Doris's old house….

''I'm not what you think I am,'' he said. ''I'm a criminal—''

''A *criminal!*'' she cried.

''I kidnapped my own daughter.''

CHAPTER FIFTEEN

"No!" Eva stared at him, horrified. *"Fanny?"*

"I've been evading the law for several years."

"The three years you've been here on the island? *That's* why you're here, isn't it? To hide out?"

"Yes." He was silent. "I regret the crime but I do not regret saving my daughter. It was the right thing to do."

"Silas!"

"I'd do it again tomorrow if I had to." His voice was bleak. Final. He stared at the ceiling. Eva didn't know what to say. All she could think of was *criminal! Kidnapper!* Had he taken Fanny from her own mother?

"Oh, Silas," she whispered. She realized she was crying.

"Do you want to know what happened?"

"Yes," she whispered. She squeezed her eyes shut, trying to stem the tears. *Did* she? Did she want to know anything more about this?

"I met Fanny's mother six years ago. Her name

was Vivian LaPre and she was from Haiti, a dancer and rather mediocre singer, with a Caribbean group. We met at a party. I had plans to go overseas for a year to study with various masters. Marrakech, Paris, Bucharest.'' Silas was silent for another long moment, as though thinking back, perhaps reliving those times in his mind. He seemed very remote. Eva shivered, although she wasn't cold, how could she be, still curled against Silas's warm body?

''I'd bought my tickets, made my arrangements and then, when I met Vivian, I decided to do a photographic portfolio of my work, a kind of visual essay with her wearing my best pieces. Modelling. We had an affair. It's a very common story, isn't it?'' He didn't wait for her response. ''I didn't ask any questions, of course. She never told me she was married—''

''Where was her husband?'' Eva asked.

''She'd left him. It was quite a complicated business. I, uh, I only found all that out when I discovered nearly three years later that I had a daughter.''

''What do you mean—*discovered?*''

Silas turned toward her. ''You believe me, don't you, when I say that Fanny means everything to me?''

Eva nodded slowly. She'd seen them together. They'd bonded in a way she'd rarely seen fathers and daughters bond. Rarely seen fathers and sons bond, for that matter, although her experience had been limited to observing families in her elementary classes. Mostly mothers and nannies came to pick children up from school, not dads….

She knew her own experience was probably skewed. Her father had always been wrapped up in his own world. Maybe Jack Haines was the exception, not Silas Lord.

"When I came back from Europe, I was determined to make some changes in my life," Silas went on. "I was twenty-seven. My father had left my mother and gone to New Zealand with a girlfriend. I'd been with a lot of women and I knew that what I was doing wasn't right. I didn't want to end up like my father. I'd make love to a woman and then I'd forget about her a week later…."

Eva shrank away from him a little; she couldn't help it. His arm tightened around her. "That's behind me, Eva. Anyway, I decided when I got back that Vivian was someone I hadn't treated well and I made up my mind to get in touch with her again and—"

"And what? *Apologize?*" Eva couldn't hide her amazement. "Don't you think a year was long enough for her to get over you?"

"Of course it was. You must think I have a very high opinion of myself." He forced a smile. "But this was something I felt I had to do. A way of redeeming myself, giving myself permission to go forward, so to speak. I'm like that, you know—'' he paused ''—I look for signs. Omens, warnings, signals that my life is about to change. Seeing you at The Baths was a sign—''

''Good, I hope,'' Eva said, too quickly.

''I knew the moment I saw you that it was a good sign. I can't explain it. It's how I decide to make a piece of jewelry. I think about the gemstone, the metal, the woman. Somewhere in there is the spark of the idea that will eventually become the piece. I trust the process.''

''So, did Vivian accept your regrets?'' Eva couldn't keep the note of disbelief from her voice, but Silas didn't seem to notice.

''Vivian had disappeared. I opened my shop in Vancouver, hired someone to run it while I put all my energy into developing my designs and working at my craft and, all the while, I kept asking about Vivian. People I knew in the entertainment world, nightclub owners, druggies. It was the world Vivian lived in. A few remembered her, but no one had seen her since maybe three or four months after I'd left for Europe. One dancer I talked to said she thought Vivian had gone back to her husband. That was the first I'd heard of any husband.''

''Why didn't you just give it up then?'' All she could think of was that the man she'd been fantasizing about for a week, the man who was now in her bed, was a *criminal.* "She'd left her husband, had an affair with you and then they got back together. These things happen all the time. Most people would've dropped it."

"Two reasons." Silas reached for the covers. Eva was glad of the quilt now. She wished she'd gotten up earlier and closed the window, too. "One, I was angry that she hadn't told me anything about any husband. I might not have had a whole lot of principles back then, but I didn't screw married women. Two, the dancer mentioned something else. She said she thought Vivian was pregnant."

Eva was silent, digesting this last bit of information. Of course—Fanny. Of course Silas had persisted. Even if he'd gotten over the fact that she hadn't come clean with him—and, really, how honest had he been with her?—he was bound to wonder about a pregnancy.

"Naturally, you assumed the child was yours." This time, Silas gave her a sharp glance.

"I did. The time frame was right. And if the baby wasn't mine, I wanted to know that, too."

"But she'd gone back to her husband. She would've had the baby. Wouldn't you assume that everything was working out for her?"

"Not necessarily," he said grimly. "She'd already left him once, remember? How did I know she was okay? I didn't have any naive ideas about the two of us getting together again, married or whatever. I didn't love her and I'm convinced she didn't love me. It was just one of those things.'' He shrugged. ''But if she'd had my baby, I wanted to make sure she had money, everything she needed. I wanted to be a father to that child, even if it was only from a distance, even if I was only a monthly check in the mail.''

''You didn't care about your son or daughter getting to know you?''

''Of course I did! But how likely was that? Vivian had hightailed it without telling me, so I guess that meant she didn't want me to know.''

''To be fair, Silas, you'd gone to Europe. How was she supposed to tell you?''

He sighed. ''Maybe. But she could've sent me a letter. Tracked me down through mutual friends. Acquaintances. She didn't want me in her baby's life, that's how it looked to me.''

''Are you bitter about that?''

''Damn right I'm bitter! But what could I do? She was an independent woman, and this was her choice. To all appearances, she'd be one more single mother. If she ever needed me, I wanted to help her, that's all. Help my child.''

Eva waited, and when Silas didn't continue, she asked softly, ''How did you find her?''

"I hired a private detective through my lawyer. He picked up Vivian's trail in Oregon. She'd connected with her husband, he played in a band or something, and they'd gone to Portland, San Francisco, Sacramento, Eugene—all over the Pacific Northwest and California."

"Doing what?"

"Oh, this and that. Song-and-dance stuff. Trying to make a living, I guess. He was an American, and that's how she got into the country, by marrying him. The music gigs would probably have been under the table."

"A-and Fanny?"

"That's where things get difficult," Silas said heavily. It was a little lighter outside now, maybe four o'clock, half-past.... A gray, predawn world.

"How?"

"The husband—I forget his name," Silas said angrily. "He didn't want Fanny. He didn't want a baby, especially one that his wife had been pregnant with before they got back together. He wanted her to have an abortion, but she wouldn't. He told her when the baby was born, it was him or the kid."

"No!" Eva was shocked.

"That's the report I got from the investigator. You know these people, they talk to everybody, neighbors, storekeepers, garbage collectors. Vivian left the bastard again when she was eight months pregnant and came back to Canada. She had Fanny in a hospital in Victoria. April 12," Silas mused. "Good Friday. An Easter baby."

"And?"

"She seems to have managed for six months on her own, then she turned Fanny over to a foster family and went to Seattle again. The P.I. lost track of her there, but it was clear she'd gone back to the husband. This was all old stuff by the time I found out about it. I didn't give a damn about Vivian by then. Or the asshole she'd married. I wanted my daughter."

"And where was she?"

"She was two years old. She was with people who had three kids of their own and were looking after three more."

"And you *kidnapped* her from them?"

"I never planned to kidnap her. I never planned to do anything. But I made the mistake, some would say," he added bitterly, and Eva wondered who had opposed him on this, "of going to see her."

THAT DAY, a Monday, Silas had driven from the ferry terminal at Swartz Bay to the small up-island town where Fanny lived. It was cold and wet but as he drove north, the weather cleared. Silas had no hidden agenda—he simply wanted to see his child with his own eyes. He'd had several photographs from the P.I., most taken from a distance.

Scott, of course, had advised against it but Silas didn't always take his good friend and lawyer's advice. He knew Scott was considering his best interests, if you could call his best interests getting out of a very difficult situation with as little expense as possible—both to the bank account and to the heart. Not that Scott was probably too concerned with the latter cost. He had the kind of attitude Silas himself might have had a few years earlier. Let sleeping dogs lie. Send money, acknowledge your responsibility if pressed, but, for God's sake, don't get involved.

But that had all changed.

The private investigator had provided a map and directions to the playground where the day care went for outdoor recreation. There was a play area—swings, a sand pit, climbing apparatus—between the Island Highway and the shore. Silas recognized it from the photographs. He parked his vehicle in the paved lot that adjoined the facility, which was obviously a community park of some kind. There were four or five vehicles in the lot.

Then he sat down on a wooden bench overlooking the playground and unfolded his newspaper. An elderly couple occupied an adjacent bench, enjoying the sun that had just peeked out of the clouds and tossing pieces of bread to gulls that swooped and screamed above. Silas felt like a damned pervert in a cap and dark glasses, sitting hunched up behind the *Globe and Mail,* spying on kids.

He caught his breath as he saw the straggle of small children approach the play area, just after ten o'clock, exactly as the detective had said. The day care catered to preschoolers and toddlers, not infants, and there appeared to be about twenty kids between two and four or five, several of them dark-skinned. Native Indians, Chinese, Guatemalans—a little half-Haitian girl? He couldn't tell from this distance.

There were two caregivers, one carrying a baby in a cloth contraption on her chest. She lugged a diaper bag and looked like she hadn't slept in a week. The other caregiver, who seemed to be about thirty, walked beside her. The two women chatted as they went, the mother stopping once to peer down at her baby and adjust something, while the children tramped on, swinging linked hands, in the time-honored "alligator" of day cares and kindergartens everywhere.

Silas snapped his paper, which had buckled in the light breeze, and observed the group carefully over the top of the editorial page. He was no expert on child care, but he would've thought the ratio of two adults to—count 'em—eighteen small kids was inadequate.

The children started to run as they neared the play area, with the caregivers calling cautions that were about as effective as the cries of the seagulls overhead. This ritual must have a mind-numbing regularity: the daily walk from the nearby day care—in a church basement, the P.I. had said—the last-minute run to secure favored spots on the swings and in the sandbox, the scoldings ignored. Even the old couple looked as though they were fixtures on the scene.

One little girl fell during the stampede. She began to wail and Silas's stomach tensed. *His* daughter? The woman with the baby bent to examine the damage and awkwardly helped the girl to her feet. No, this child had red hair.

One child stopped by the climbing apparatus and looked directly at him. A boy. Silas's heart fell again. He decided to turn the page and feigned interest in the letters to the editor for a few minutes. Then another child looked his way and this time—dear God!—it was his daughter.

It had to be. The photo the P.I. had given him, grainy or not, was of this girl. She had on a sweatshirt with a hood, blue or green, and the hood had fallen off to reveal masses of dark curls. She had big brown eyes and she was staring straight at him.

She started toward him—no, it was the elderly couple she was approaching, her hands up in the air to mimic the birds. The caregiver who seemed to be in charge, the one without the infant, called her back—''Fanny!'' That was the clincher. Reluctantly, the girl turned. Already Silas felt an insane kind of pride. He could sense her determination to get on the climbing equipment, which bristled with little boys, while several children quarreled over the four seats available on the swing set.

The elderly couple got up to leave, shaking the last of the crumbs from the brown paper bag. The old man carefully folded it and stowed it in his trouser pocket, and then the two of them strolled toward the water. There was a boardwalk that ran the length of the beach; Silas had noticed it earlier.

Distracted, Silas glanced back at the children in time to see a situation developing, the situation that would give him his daughter. A child fell off the swing set after a particularly enthusiastic push from one of the older children, a four- or five-year old, who immediately hopped onto the empty seat. When the girl who'd fallen got up, she was crying and walked straight into the oncoming path of another swing, which walloped her and knocked her off her feet again. Several children started yelling and the caregiver in charge rushed to the scene of the accident. The child who'd been hit screamed blue murder but Silas couldn't see any blood and she obviously hadn't been knocked out.

Then he saw Fanny leave the play area again and walk toward him, raising her arms to swoop like the seagulls, which still filled the air with piercing cries as they wheeled, perhaps aware only now that their free lunch was over.

It was surreal. This couldn't be happening, Silas thought as the child continued toward him, oblivious to anything except the birds and her own peculiar dance.

Everything seemed to happen at once. The caregiver in charge shouted something to the other one and then hurried toward a small outbuilding Silas had also noticed earlier, possibly washroom facilities for the park. A cluster of three children accompanied her, including the child who'd been hit by the swing.

For some reason, the new mother decided at that time to remove her baby from the cloth carrier and it began to scream. Silas realized she was putting the infant down on a blanket on the grass, and that a knot of interested children had crowded around the baby and mother, screening him from her view, although she could hardly have seen him anyway, turned away as she was, tending to her squalling infant. Silas had no idea where the other caregiver had gone—or when she'd be back.

But there was his daughter—his Fanny!—right in front of him, smiling. He thrust the newspaper into the trash can beside the bench and held out his arms. She came straight toward him.

Silas believed God would strike him down before he reached his car with the child in his arms. Surely someone had noticed! The old couple, one of the caregivers, a passerby, *someone* would call the authorities and he'd be picked up before he could exit the parking lot.

Nothing happened. Fanny didn't say boo. Perhaps she'd had so many adults looking after her in her short life, she simply believed he was another one. He strapped her into the back seat of the Blazer, willing himself not to look around, certain half a dozen tough-looking cops had materialized from the bushes and were watching every move he made. His brain was churning; he had no plan.

He dumped the coins onto the floor from the small, bright-yellow plastic bin he used for parking change and handed it to the child. Something she could play with while he drove—where?

Liberty Island. The old Lord place. No one had lived there for years. No one would find them there.

The plastic bucket prompted a sunny smile and the first word he'd heard from his daughter. ''T'a!''

Silas knew he'd treasure that moment until the end of his days.

CHAPTER SIXTEEN

THE SUN SHONE brilliantly into the small bedroom the next time Eva woke. She had no idea what time it might be, but it *felt* late. Her watch was on the bedside table where she'd put it the night before, when she'd climbed into bed and fallen asleep to the sound of the storm raging outside. She didn't want to risk waking Silas by leaning over him to check the time.

What did it matter anyway?

For a few minutes, she lay there staring at the square of blue sky through the bare window. She could hear morning birds chirruping loudly and the occasional clump-clump of Andy's hooves against the door of his box stall. He hated being penned up. From somewhere in the distance was the reassuring buzz of boat motors. Sound traveled over the water, especially after a storm.

What a story. What a predicament. What an extraordinary night.

When Silas had finished relating his strange story, he'd made love to her with a passion and tenderness that had taken her breath. She cared for him deeply. She couldn't help it. It was something that just—just *was.* It had nothing to so with what had happened last night. She would never have allowed him into her bed unless she'd felt the way she did.

Could she be so sure of that? She'd been thinking about him every day and every night since she'd met him. Some of her obsession had to be due to the isolation. The fact that there was so little to occupy the mind. There was no television—Eva hadn't fired up the generator and didn't intend to—and even radio reception was uncertain. Then there was the obvious: Silas's presence on the island fit with the dashing, romantic picture she and her sisters had built up so many summers ago, when they weren't much more than Fanny's age. Childish, perhaps, but still a factor.

She'd tried to forget him over the past week. She'd read the paperback she'd brought with her but hadn't been able to drum up much interest in the shelves of damp-spotted and mildewed books on Doris's shelves, mostly pre-World War Two editions of forgotten authors writing forgettable stories. She'd leafed through several, had ended up with a sneezing fit and given up.

Her mind had constantly returned to the only really interesting things she'd discovered on this island—Silas and his daughter, Fanny. Many of her questions had now been answered, at least from Silas's viewpoint. The vagueness, the secrecy, the reluctance to answer what she felt were ordinary questions about school and playmates, the way Silas had shuffled her off to the house to have her foot attended to when Fanny was too forthcoming, the initial caution of the housekeeper with her low-voiced queries about Doris's health.

Now that she knew Silas was a fugitive, harboring his kidnapped daughter on Liberty Island with the aid and complicity of the old couple, much of that mystery had been revealed. From Silas's point of view, she reminded herself.

Indeed, she could see that Silas must have regarded her unexpected appearance on the island as a threat. His goal, as he'd stated to her the night he'd walked her back from the barbecue, was to own the whole island. To be truly lord of his domain.

So why had he told her all this?

How could he possibly trust her enough to confess so many details? So many *incriminating* details, if she was ever interviewed by the police, heaven forbid. Didn't he realize that she couldn't possibly go along with what he'd done?

Impulse was one thing, maybe even understandable considering his unusual, even desperate circumstances, but to continue to hide his daughter here on Liberty Island? For *years?* How long did he intend to go on doing that? It was simply wrong. Fanny needed to be with other children. She needed to go to school. Now Eva understood the strange comment about "children in books." They were the only children Fanny knew.

As a trained teacher and an advocate for children, Eva should have been the last person Silas confided in. Unless...unless what?

It didn't make sense. At least not this morning and not to her calm, rational mind. Last night it had been part of their closeness, the sudden and intense intimacy in the midst of the storm, the sharing of their minds and spirits and bodies that went with—well, with good sex. Silas was an accomplished lover. The intensity of his lovemaking combined with the sweetness and sensitivity with which he'd enfolded her in his arms, kissing her softly before they slept. She'd never forget it. By his own admission, he'd had lots of practice, but Eva knew she ought to discount that factor, considering the emotional swamp she'd suddenly found herself in. That was going to be hard.

She believed him. She believed *in* him. It would be very hard to decide what to do next.

"*A-HOY!* Ahoy there this house!"

Eva suddenly realized that the general boating noises she'd heard through the partially open window had come nearer—much nearer—and there was the unmistakable sound of a vessel nudging up to the wharf, its motors suddenly reversing, the burble and gasp of the backwash swirling over propellers....

"You expecting company?" Silas was instantly awake, and his smile dispelled the alarm bells that had been hammering away at her brain. Where was the hunted look he'd had last night? This man was rested, relaxed...sexy.

"No." He kissed her into silence and swung his legs over the side of the narrow bed. "Time for me to vamoose." He grinned. "Can't have visitors finding the lady of the manor in bed with the bad boy from next door."

"Ahoy there! Eva? *Anybody home?*"

Eva pushed the window open wider and wrapped the top sheet around her before kneeling on the cot and peering out, only her head and shoulders revealed.

"Dad!"

Her shock must have communicated itself to Silas, who laughed, grabbed his shirt and pulled it over his head. He'd already managed to get into his jeans. Socks? Shoes? Underwear? They must be somewhere, littered about the tiny bedroom. Silas headed for the top of the stairs. "I'll, uh, take the back door. I feel like a teenager sleeping at his girlfriend's house and then the parents get home early from their weekend at the lake.'' He grinned again and Eva felt a surge of laughter. This wasn't shocking, this was *crazy!*

She jumped up, still wrapped in the sheet, and ran to him at the top of the stairs and kissed him until they were both laughing. Eva could hear her father banging away on the kitchen door downstairs.

''Quick!'' She grabbed her robe and shrugged it on, following Silas down the narrow stairs, pushing him as she went. ''Hurry! *Hurry!*''

Eva raced for the kitchen door, glad she'd locked it against the wind last night. Before she unlatched it, she glanced over her shoulder in time to see Silas disappear out the French doors that led to the patio. One of the doors was still blocked by the chest in front of the broken panes.

''Dad! What a surprise!''

''Sleeping on the job, are you? Ha-ha. Well...'' Jack Haines glanced at his watch. He was wearing khaki shorts, a striped T-shirt and his old boating cap. ''I guess it *is* just half-past eight. We stayed over at Secret Cove last night out of that blow and thought we'd have our breakfast here with you this morning. Little family party!''

''We?'' Eva cinched her robe around her waist, then stepped forward in bare feet to give her father a hug. He responded, as always, briefly and awkwardly. *As though she were a stranger.* Eva could hear Andy braying in the woodshed and the sharp yap-yap of a dog. Freddie, presumably. "I'd better let that donkey out," she finished in a mutter. She hoped Silas had made his escape, unseen, while they were busy at the kitchen door.

"The girls. Sue Ellen and her friend, Monica. The pair of them are staying with me for ten days—"

"With *you?*" Eva was surprised. Sue Ellen was Leona's eldest. Her sister must have mellowed. There was a time she wouldn't have allowed Jack Haines to keep an eye on one of her ostrich eggs, never mind her precious children.

"We're sailing up to Desolation Sound."

"Grandpa, Grandpa! There's a *donkey* out there in the shed—oh, hi, Aunt Eva." Sue Ellen came flying around the corner of the house, her little bespectacled friend beside her, and Jack's dachshund galloping madly behind them.

"Hi yourself," Eva responded, stepping forward and giving the sturdy blond girl a hug. "And this must be your friend, Monica, Grandpa was telling me about." She smiled at the other child, a thin brunette who kept nervously pushing her glasses up on the bridge of her nose. "Why don't you let Andy out, Sue Ellen? He doesn't like being stuck inside on such a nice morning."

"Oh, boy! Can we?" The girls tore off again and Eva invited her father inside.

"I'm just going to run up and get dressed, Dad. You rummage around in the fridge, see what you can find for breakfast. I'm afraid I'm not that well stocked." Eva went upstairs, marveling at this turn of events. Thank goodness Silas had gotten away. What an absurd predicament! No romance in her life for months and months and the one time there's a man in her bed, her father happens to drop by for a visit! Of course, she wasn't seventeen anymore. Not, she reflected, that Jack Haines would've said anything then, either. He'd always prided himself on being what he called "modern." Eva often felt he was a lot more "modern" in his thinking than his daughters were or than his daughters would have liked him to be. Never mind, she thought as she pulled on a clean orange T-shirt and some terry cloth shorts. The past was history. She rummaged around for a clean pair of socks. She would've liked a shower, too, but was going to have to wait until later for a swim.

With Silas and Fanny? And the rest of the crew? And Bruno and Freddie? That would be *too* amazing.

It turned out to be that kind of day. Eva managed to put together a decent breakfast for her guests, with coffee and orange juice, ham and omelettes from her provisions and fresh croissants from the Secret Cove store, contributed by her father. They lingered over coffee while the girls explored, even climbing up into the tree house Eva and her sisters had practically lived in during their summer visits. The tree house was dilapidated but still usable, according to Sue Ellen and Monica.

''Did you see Doris?'' Eva asked. She'd discovered that her father and the girls had already spent three days meandering up the coast in Jack's old thirty-five-foot motor-sailer, the *Jack-in-the-Box.* Traditionally, most boats were named for women—as was Doris's old runabout, the *Edie B.,* named by her husband for his sister Edith Bonhomme. But that wasn't Eva's father's style. Tradition? What was tradition? He'd named his boat after himself.

''I'll see her on our return trip,'' Jack replied. He stood suddenly and picked up his plate and cup. ''Now, what I really want to do today is help you deal with all this—this garbage.'' He waved dismissively around Doris's garden, including her house in his gesture. ''I've been feeling a tad guilty that you've been spending your summer vacation like this while I've been whiling away my days reading the paper and improving my tan. Ha-ha!''

Of course, the last thing Jack Haines would do was spend time ''improving'' his tan; that, Eva knew, was his idea of a joke. She was grateful, nonetheless, for his offer of help.

They spent the rest of the morning packing boxes. Jack pushed away the chest Silas had wedged in front of the broken panes of glass in order to sweep away the broken glass and temporarily repair the gaping hole with cardboard and tape.

"Oh, ho! What's this?" Jack had said when he'd moved the chest into the center of the room. At the back of the chest, behind a foreshortened drawer, was wedged an antique wooden music box. The silver-lined but now badly tarnished lower portion of the box held a scene painted on porcelain and the old mechanism actually still worked, playing a tinny version of some music Eva didn't recognize.

"I'll take this to Doris," she said, running her finger over the dusty surface, which looked like rosewood. The box was deep, as though possibly containing a drawer or storage area, but Eva could find no way to get open it. Doris might remember. She set the music box aside to take to Sechelt on her next trip.

Her father had started another bonfire and Eva had just come out onto the patio with a pot of tea and two mugs when Silas and Fanny appeared at the ramshackle fence.

Before Eva could hurry forward, Jack had gone to the fence and opened the sagging gate. Eva took a few steps toward them, hoping her face wouldn't betray her.

"I'm Silas Lord," she heard Silas say, offering his hand to her father. "I'm, uh—" his gaze caught hers and Eva sincerely hoped he wasn't going to continue with "—sleeping with your daughter."

He didn't. He shook her father's hand and said, "I'm here to help."

CHAPTER SEVENTEEN

"AND THIS IS my daughter, Fanny," Silas murmured.

So this man was Eva's father.

Silas had expected someone more...well, substantial. The stereotype of a banker or a corporate vice president. Or a well-fed salesman-type, possibly. This man was tall and lean, with buzz-cut gray hair and a day's growth on his chin, and he had a light in his eye that Silas had not expected to see. It was the light of the wanderer, or the malcontent. Or the mad scientist?

"Your daughter, is it? Aha!" The sharp blue eyes narrowed for just a moment as they fastened on Fanny. Silas wasn't used to people meeting him and Fanny, so he was somewhat taken aback at the sudden focus. Old fears flared up—would they be recognized? To be fair to Eva's father, Silas knew they hardly looked like the typical Canadian father and daughter, him with his mother's Swedish blue eyes and sandy brown hair and Fanny with her warm brown skin and mass of black curls.

"Have you got kids?" Fanny asked immediately. Silas tensed. It had been a risk bringing her. But he'd felt compelled to widen her circle, even the tiniest bit. Jack Haines was an outsider, but he was also Eva's father. And, since Silas had confessed everything to Eva—he still wasn't sure exactly *why* he had—he supposed it didn't matter if her father met Fanny. Three years was a long time and there'd been nothing from the law. Nothing from Vivian. Perhaps it was time to relax a little.

Jack Haines laughed. "Yes, I do. Eva's my kid. And if you want to meet one of my *grand*-kids, she's in a tree house out back—" he waved and pointed "—with her friend Monica."

"Can I go see them, Daddy?" She gazed up at him, her eyes a mixture of trepidation and excitement. "Please!" She jumped up and down, still clinging to his hand.

"How old is your granddaughter, Mr. Haines?" Silas was incredibly aware of Eva. She'd come a little closer, then had gone back to the patio, where she was waiting with a tray in her hands. He could tell how nervous she was. So was he. As soon as he'd gotten home and had time to shower and change, he'd been scheming ways to return. Offering to help was an obvious excuse. That, and finding the garnet necklace in Fanny's stash…

"I insist you call me Jack," Eva's father said to

him, then turned to Fanny. "Sue Ellen's ten. Her little friend is, er, oh, I don't know, about the same, I guess. Go ahead. Go have fun. That's what childhood's for!"

Silas nodded at his daughter, giving her permission, and Fanny left on a flat run, Bruno shambling behind her. "I know where the tree house is, Dad!" she shouted over her shoulder. "Eva showed me."

"Ah," said the older man, turning toward the patio and gesturing for Silas to accompany him, "you're familiar with the place, are you? I wondered, you being a Lord and all."

"I've been here once or twice since your daughter arrived," Silas answered noncommittally. "My daughter's been here a few times."

"Hello, Silas," Eva said when they got to the sitting area of the patio. She'd set down the tray and was looking delightfully bothered. Her eyes were very conscious of him. "You've met my father, I see. Would you like some tea? I'll just go get another cup." She disappeared into the house without waiting for his reply.

"Don't suppose that would've happened when my wife's cousin was living here," Jack went on. He fixed Silas with a very bright eye as he grabbed a cookie off the plate Eva had set out and took a bite. "You just visiting, I mean."

"No." Silas pulled out a chair. "Your cousin was not particularly fond of me or my family."

"Oh-ho!" Jack Haines snorted with laughter. "That's putting it nicely, young man. She couldn't bear the idea of the Lords' very existence, is what you mean."

"What are you going on about, Dad?" Eva had come back, holding a third mug, and was looking more composed. She even managed a small smile for him, which Silas returned.

"Oh, Doris! And all that nonsense about her neighbors." Jack Haines reached for another cookie.

"But why, Dad? Did you ever know what that was all about?"

Jack shrugged. "Who knows for sure, Eva? It's all foolishness. You ever see that movie *Cold Comfort Farm*? You should. People do strange things. Listen, could you pour me some tea, Eva? I'm going to go down and keep an eye on the fire." Silas could see the skeleton of a chair gradually turning to ash in the midst of the flames. The older man picked up his mug and looked at him again. "So—up at the island for the summer, are you?" he asked sociably.

Silas didn't miss a beat. "Something like that, sir."

"Jack!" Eva's father gesticulated with his mug, slopping tea over the side. "I won't be called 'Mr.

Haines' or 'sir' anymore, not since I left the classroom behind and that's a good many years ago.''

Silas watched him make his way to the fire pit. *Interesting old guy.* ''How long?''

''Since he quit teaching?'' Eva asked, pouring tea into the other mugs. ''Quite a while. He's sixty-seven and he retired early, at fifty-five. He liked teaching and he liked literature—that was his subject, English and French—but he hated the university.''

''Are you the youngest?'' Silas asked, adding milk to his tea. ''After last night, I feel I know you so well. And yet I really know almost nothing about you. Except that you're a teacher, too.''

''Yes.'' Eva's voice trembled. ''I—I almost can't believe that last night happened....''

''Believe it,'' he told her.

She nodded. Her eyes sought and held his.

He wanted to take her in his arms and kiss her and lead her upstairs and start the night all over again.

''I do believe it. It was wonderful. It just seems so—so strange to have you arrive now and meet my dad and sit down for tea and...all that.''

''Which reminds me,'' Silas said, digging in his jeans pocket and pulling out an envelope. ''I brought something for you. Really for your cousin, I guess.''

''What is it?'' Eva leaned forward and Silas

spilled the silver-and-garnet necklace onto the rusted cast iron tabletop. "Oh, my goodness!"

"I found it in the stuff you sent over with Fanny. Of course, she can't keep anything like that. I cleaned it up some—it was very badly tarnished. I'm not surprised you didn't think it had any value."

Eva picked up the necklace and examined it. Silas watched as the intricately worked chain intertwined with her fingers—slim, brown from the sun, with short, sensibly cut nails. She had beautiful hands. Capable hands. He'd meant everything he'd said last night—she was the most beautiful woman he'd ever met, in every way.

"I believe there's a pair of earrings that match this. Fanny didn't want them. What do you think it's worth?"

"Three, four thousand—"

"My goodness!" She looked shocked.

"Possibly more. It's German, I think, dating from the thirties or forties. Austrian, maybe. It might be worth more to a collector, especially if there are matching earrings. And I suppose it has some sentimental value to your cousin."

"But why would she just have left it here in the house? In among all that other junk? I don't suppose you found anything else of value?"

Silas shook his head. "No. The rest of the stuff Fanny brought home wouldn't be worth more than ten dollars. I have no idea why she'd put a valuable necklace like this in with costume jewelry. Face it, Eva, your cousin is a strange woman.''

''She's not! It's just this silliness about your family and your side of the island, that's all.''

''I rest my case,'' Silas said, smiling.

''I'm going to put it with the music box Dad found in the back of that old chest you moved last night and take it to Doris next time I go over.''

''Music box?''

''Come in,'' she said, with a sideways glance, gathering up the tea tray, ''and I'll show you.''

OF COURSE, that had just been a ruse to get him inside, away from the eyes of her father and, possibly, the girls. They'd kissed and kissed and Silas had practically made love to her on the moth-eaten sofa in the music room. She couldn't even remember if she'd actually shown him the music box.

That was the beginning of the most wonderful week of Eva's life. They'd all gone to The Baths that afternoon, the three girls, Silas and Eva, and the two dogs. Her father had stayed behind, insisting he had to take care of some small task on the *Jack-in-the-Box.* After splashing around in the three pools, mainly the first and second, for half an hour, Sue Ellen and Monica announced that they were going to Fanny's caravan. Off they trooped, both dogs following them, although a dachshund that stood maybe ten inches at the shoulder was a comical companion to a Newfoundland standing nearly three feet. After they'd gone, Silas led Eva to a place not far from The Baths, under a big cedar tree, and they spread out their towels and made love. Eva didn't think she could possibly have been happier.

The next day, after Jack and the girls had left for Desolation Sound, and Fanny was sulking in her room because she hadn't been allowed to go along, Silas took Eva to his studio and showed her the pieces he was working on.

She tried on the unfinished tanzanite bracelet and then some earrings he was making for his mother's birthday. "Topaz," he said. "My mother is a topaz woman."

"What am I?" she asked playfully, and was surprised to see how serious he became.

"You're amber," he said. "Silver and amber. I have something I'd like to show you someday."

"Why not show me now?" she asked, taking off the bracelet and handing it back to him. She watched as he replaced it in a small safe at the back of the room. His studio was in the kitchen-dining area of the little house.

"Because I'm not finished. It has to be exactly right when I show you." He came forward and took both her hands in his. "But there's something in this house I haven't shown you yet...."

"Oh?"

"Upstairs are two very private bedrooms. No one ever disturbs me here. Would you like to see them?"

"Well," Eva said, knowing her cheeks were pink and unable to do anything about it, "maybe *one* of them."

Midweek, Eva received several phone calls on her cell when the Sunshine Coast papers came out. Two were from kids, who couldn't possibly look after Andy properly, and besides, they lived in town. One was from a couple who lived near Pender Harbor and had a number of other unusual animals, including llamas and Vietnamese pigs. That was a possibility. Even more interesting was a retired army colonel who ran a children's petting zoo in Davis Bay, along with his spinster sister, a retired nurse. He said they got school groups year-round and tourists in the summer stopping by to admire the animals. Eva could see Andy being cosseted and petted by schoolchildren. He'd spent most of his life in near isolation, just an old woman and a few mythical goats to keep him company. He deserved a pampered retirement.

Silas accompanied her to the mainland to check out the prospects. Fanny didn't mind being left behind, although Eva realized that was mainly because she rarely left Liberty Island, except for the fishing and camping trips, when Silas took her in his private plane. Eva was beginning to get an inkling of how really restricted Fanny's life had become. It worried her.

She and Silas had lunch at the Garden Bay Hotel restaurant, overlooking the harbor, and then she poked through some gift shops just off the wharf, buying locally made stationery for Mrs. Klassen and a stuffed toy ladybug for Fanny. She wanted to include Matthew but had no idea what he'd like. In the end, she got him a crystal sun catcher to hang in his workshop window.

The petting zoo seemed the better of the two prospects and the colonel said he'd make arrangements to pick Andy up the following week. Now that she was taking some action to find a home for the donkey, she hated to see him go. It would be lonely without him.

The next day, Silas took Fanny and Eva flying, and the day after that, they went fishing in his cruiser. No one caught anything, but no one cared, either. They ate their picnic lunch on a rocky deserted islet and Bruno retrieved sticks from the water as Silas threw them, to Fanny's endless delight.

It was an idyllic week but at the end of it, Eva felt more confused than ever. Fanny adored her father; there was no question of that. And the sun in

Silas's world rose and set on the little girl. If he was arrested, what would happen to Fanny? Would she be put back in foster care? She had no mother, at least none anyone could locate. And, besides, Vivian had already largely relinquished her motherhood by abandoning Fanny and then disappearing. Yet Fanny should be going to kindergarten this fall. She should have playmates, friends her own age. A neighborhood. A community.

There was only one thing Eva knew for certain by the week's end: She was head over heels in love with Silas Lord.

CHAPTER EIGHTEEN

ON FRIDAY, Silas offered to help transport the considerable amount of discarded goods Eva had organized over the week. The *Windjammer* was much larger and more stable than the *Edie B.* and could take on more cargo. Eva's experience with clearing out Doris's house had convinced her of the virtue of getting rid of stuff as she went through life, not saving everything, including string and paper grocery bags, "just in case."

With Matthew's help, they loaded the cruiser at Doris's sagging wharf.

"I could probably even get Andy aboard if you want," Silas said when they were nearly ready to cast off. "When's he supposed to go to the petting farm?"

"Next week sometime. I'll call the colonel and see if he's made arrangements already." Silas's offer was welcome. The colonel had said he'd look into arranging transport, but Eva could tell he wasn't a seafaring man and probably had no idea where to start with the job of removing a donkey from an island. It would be risky trying to get Andy into the *Edie B,* as she'd considered doing. Even properly haltered and restrained, the donkey could cause her a lot of grief if he decided to struggle. He might even tip the boat.

After making two trips in the truck from Half Moon Bay to Sechelt and back again to get rid of a dozen boxes and various pieces of furniture, including the chest that had been in the music room, Eva dropped Silas off at the Half Moon Bay wharf. He would take the *Windjammer* back to Liberty Island, then return for her that evening. Eva had some errands to run, plus she wanted to deliver the music box and the necklace to her cousin. Eva invited Silas to accompany her but he flatly refused.

"Upset that sweet old lady all over again?" He grinned. "No way. I'll pick you up at eight. Bye, darlin'." He kissed her and was gone.

Actually, Eva entertained sentimental visions of healing the rift between the Lord family and her elderly cousin by showing up with Silas. Maybe he was right, though. When the time was right, Eva would have to break the idea gently to Doris. What idea? That she—Eva—now had a Lord in her life?

But did she? Silas had said nothing about the future.

Eva also planned to have dinner with Doris again. She felt she'd been neglecting her. She'd promised Doris she'd take care of everything on the island for her, not just the packing up, but looking into the marine trust situation, as well. Instead, in the past week, she'd spent every possible minute with Silas.

The fact that Silas had said nothing about her expected departure was troubling. Did they have a relationship, or was she just fooling herself? Maybe this was strictly a summer romance? From his perspective, anyway. The kind of sudden, hot affair stoked by sunshine and lazy days that amounted to very little when the holiday was over. Eva didn't know. Nothing like this had ever happened to her.

On the one hand, she'd be devastated if that was Silas's view. On the other hand, maybe she'd be relieved. The truth was, Eva was afraid of what loving Silas and possibly having a future with him would mean. What about the plans she'd laid out for herself? A full-time teaching job, perhaps buying an apartment or a house when she'd saved enough, falling in love—someday—with an ordinary, suitable man. Someone reliable and yes, maybe even a little bit boring. Like her.

When she was with Silas, when she was in his arms, she couldn't imagine being anywhere else. Ever.

But did she want to spend the next few years of her life hiding out on Liberty Island with a stepdaughter who'd been kidnapped and a husband on the run from the law?

A husband! Good heavens. She was getting *very*

far ahead of herself. Eva pulled into the paved lot adjacent to Seaview Lodge. It was a beautiful, calm afternoon, and groups of elderly residents were enjoying the heat of the early August sun in the manicured gardens that surrounded the lodge. Some sat on park benches, some were strolling, others were in wheelchairs with attendants. All wore sun hats and many had on dark glasses.

Doris Bonhomme was sitting on a park bench overlooking Trail Bay, a cane resting at her side. She was alone.

Eva stole up behind her, carrying the shopping bag with the music box. "Surprise!" she said as she sat down next to her. Today, Doris looked every year her age and more. She'd always had a lively manner, which had made her seem younger and perhaps more capable than she really was, but her skin was papery and frail-looking in the unforgiving light, etched with veins throbbing near the surface. Her hands were curved and knobby on the handle of the cane, her lips thin and pale, her eyebrows mannish and overgrown.

Where was the beauty of the forties and fifties? Eva had seen studio shots of Doris Bonhomme in her youth, and she'd been a remarkable-looking woman. Talented and beautiful, with a husband who'd adored her, according to Eva's mother, who'd remembered Charles Bonhomme slightly. He'd died when Doris was in her late thirties and, to the amazement of her friends and relatives, the widow had continued living on the island settled by her father-in-law at the turn of the century. Eva wasn't surprised; Doris was both loyal and stubborn.

"Ah, there you are," Doris said with a smile. She took off her dark glasses. "I'd been wondering why I haven't seen you lately."

"I've been busy. Dad showed up last week with one of Leona's girls and—"

"He did?"

Eva nodded. "And Sue Ellen brought a friend."

"Visitors! How I always loved to see people come to Liberty Island. Did they stay long?"

"Just overnight. Then they were off to Desolation Sound. They'll be back soon. I'm surprised Leona let Sue Ellen spend two weeks with Dad."

"Oh, don't be too hard on him. Jack wasn't much of a father when you girls were younger, I know that, but a man can change. Some men aren't fond of babies and very young children, that's all. You can't hold it against them forever."

"You could be right. Dad gets along fine with Sue Ellen and her friend." It was true; Jack seemed delighted to spend time with the two girls, eager to show them how to do things—fish for sand dabs, sail, look for mussels and crabs. Eva smiled and leaned over to pat Doris's knee. "I thought I'd have dinner with you this evening, if you're not otherwise engaged."

"Oh, you know I'm not." She gripped the cane in one hand and waved it toward the lowering sun over the bay. "Nothing much changes around here." She paused, then continued. "I rather like that, I've discovered. I've had enough change in my life."

"Good." Eva put the shopping bag on the bench between them.

"What have you got there?"

"Something Dad found. You might like it for your room." Eva rummaged in the bag. "And something else, something rather valuable that I'm sure you'd misplaced."

"Nonsense." Doris looked affronted. "There's nothing left in that house that I want. I've moved on, Eva. The past is behind me." Eva doubted it very much, considering what Doris had said on her last visit about never selling to a member of the Lord family. "I told your father what I required back in April and he had Bernice McTavish fetch my things." Bernice was married to Owen McTavish, the farmer who'd taken care of Andy after Doris's accident.

"Well, she wouldn't have been able to find *this,*" Eva said triumphantly, pulling the music box from the bag. "It was stuffed behind a drawer in—"

"*Where* did you get that?" Doris's already pale face went white. Her eyes widened and she put one hand to her chest.

"Oh, my goodness." Eva thrust the music box back in the shopping bag, suddenly worried. "Doris! Are you okay?"

"I'm all right," came the whispered reply. If there was such a thing as seeing a ghost, Doris had seen one. She stared at the shopping bag.

"'Fondly I'm dreaming, ever of thee,'" she quoted softly, apropos of nothing. Then she was silent for a few seconds. "Where did you say you found it?"

"It was in a chest in the music room," Eva explained. "Behind a drawer that had been altered."

"I see." Doris's stare was distant, unfocused. "What else have you got?"

"Just this." Eva took the music box out of the bag again and opened the lid. There was a mirror fitted inside the lid, bevelled and brilliant, showing no effects of time, but the rest of the interior, except for the medallion that was inset into the bottom of the cavity was blackened and tarnished. The scene painted on the porcelain medallion was an old-fashioned, rather commonplace subject: two young men in top hats and black coats reclining on a lawn beneath a tree, a young woman in a bonnet and long dress tending to the contents of a bountiful picnic basket, plates and bottles and teacups spread around her on an embroidered cloth.

Eva had tucked the necklace, still in the manila envelope Silas had brought it in, inside the cavity of the music box. She opened the envelope and spilled the necklace into her hand. Doris's expression didn't change. Eva held it toward her and, for a long moment, Doris stared at the necklace, as though Eva's palm held a cluster of bees. Tentatively, she reached out and touched it with one gnarled trembling finger. Then, as Eva watched, barely breathing, Doris took it from her. "It's been polished," she said.

"Yes." Eva refrained from admitting who'd been responsible not only for discovering the necklace but cleaning it.

Doris examined the silver chain and pendant, touching each dark-red stone. "There are earrings to this somewhere."

"Yes, I know. I haven't had a chance to clean them yet. I thought I'd see if you wanted them."

"My husband was buried on the island, you know."

"No!" Eva was shocked. "Where?"

"Above the dam. On Abel's Peak. With the goats." The dam was the old weir that had been built near the source of the creek to supply fresh water to the Bonhomme and Lord households via a wooden aqueduct, replaced sometime in the past fifty years with galvanized piping.

"When you have loved with all your heart, you cannot imagine loving someone else exactly as much. That is a woman's folly, you know. But it can happen. I am not referring to loving a child," she said, turning to Eva and regarding her somewhat severely. "I had no children. I am referring to loving a man. A *husband. Two* men."

Eva caught her breath. What did Doris mean? Was this the tragedy of her life? That she'd loved once, only to be disappointed? Perhaps her first love had died—of tuberculosis or in a duel of honor or on a battlefield in France. And had she then found happiness with Charles Bonhomme, perhaps felt guilty about it?

"Of course," Doris continued dismissively, returning to her original topic, "you can't bury people just anywhere these days. Back then you could do as you pleased. It was all properly done, with a minister attending, of course. My husband was very particular and that was his wish. If I want to be buried beside him, I expect I'll have to be cremated first and then maybe you can dig a hole and—"

"Doris! Let's not talk about that. Your hip's healed nicely, and you've got a good many years ahead of you."

"I hope not. Not at this place, satisfactory though it is." She held the necklace out to Eva. "Will you fasten this for me? I believe I'll wear it now."

Eva fastened the necklace around Doris's wrinkled neck and gave her a hug. "It looks lovely on you!"

"Yes," Doris agreed matter-of-factly, glancing down at the old-fashioned piece and smoothing it against the creased and freckled skin of her throat and breast, "it always did. Is it nearly time for dinner?"

Eva checked her watch. "Very soon."

Her cousin reached for the music box and Eva set it on her knees. The old woman gazed out at the bay, her arms securely around the rosewood box, and after a moment she lifted the lid and pressed something. The music began. "'Years have not chill'd the love I cherish, True as the stars hath my heart been to thee,'" Doris sang in a soft, quavery voice while Eva fumbled blindly for a tissue in her bag.

"'Ah! Never till life and mem'ry perish, Can I forget how dear thou art to me—'"

Oh, Eva thought as she blew her nose once, then again, loudly, *I am such a sentimental fool!*

"'—Morn, noon and night, Where e'er I may be,'" Doris sang on, her voice gathering strength, "'Fondly I'm dreaming, ever of thee!'"

CHAPTER NINETEEN

WHEN EVA GOT TO the Half Moon Bay wharf at half-past seven to meet Silas, he was waiting for her, accompanied by a pale man whom he introduced as the Klassens' son, Ivor.

Ivor was tall, like his father, and very quiet. Eva didn't think he said a word during the entire half hour of the crossing. He sat up in the cockpit with Silas and stared out at the islands they passed, his hair blowing in the wind. He had a vacant, sleepy look that Eva presumed was a symptom of the head injury he'd suffered as a boy.

How sad for the Klassens! And, of course, for Ivor. Eva didn't know any details of the accident, only what Doris had told her on the previous visit.

She was feeling rather sad herself. Her cousin's reaction to the music box and necklace had affected Eva deeply. They'd had a quiet meal together and then Doris wanted to go to her room. To rest, she said apologetically. It was a gentle reminder to Eva that her cousin preferred to be alone. With her thoughts, with the ghosts of her memories.

Of the two young men she'd loved. Doris had said nothing more about either her husband or her mysterious first love, but Eva hadn't needed details to piece together an elaborate romantic story. She couldn't wait to pester her father for particulars. He *must* know more than he'd let on.

Silas invited her to join them for the evening, a sort of alternative to the postponed Friday-evening dinner, which Eva had heard about from Mrs. Klassen in the Bluebird Bakery—was it really only a week ago?—but Eva declined. She couldn't face making small talk or playing dominoes with a silent stranger and felt that her presence might simply dampen the get-together. Ivor appeared to be as much a part of Silas's family as his daughter and the Klassens. She—Eva—would be the outsider.

She avoided Silas's searching gaze when she told him she'd rather go straight home and was glad he accepted her decision without further question. The fact was, she wanted to be alone, too. After Jack's visit with the two girls, plus the intense, emotionally exhausting week she'd spent with Silas, plus all the packing-up activity, Eva just felt weary and wanted to think things over. So much had happened in such a short time.

The house was even drearier than it'd been when she first arrived. She'd gotten used to it. But now, coming back from the mainland, with so much furniture moved out or destroyed, so many drawers emptied and closets bare, the house really did feel strange. Even Andy seemed out of sorts. He nuzzled her pocket for treats, and then, when she ran out of chunks of carrot for him, he bared his teeth in a large yellow display of irritation and trotted off to begin cropping the sparse grass along the beach.

She was going to miss him.

Maybe by the time he left next week, she'd be ready to go, too. She could be finished if she worked hard. Her father was returning from Desolation Sound about then. Maybe one last family goodbye to the old homestead, the site of so many happy memories, and then they could all sail away, leaving the marine trust to decide what to do next with the Bonhomme property.

She knew that when she left she'd probably never see Silas Lord again. She wished he'd never told her about abducting Fanny. She wished he'd never told her about his affair with Vivian LaPre. She wished she had someone she could talk to about…about everything.

Eva had a restless night. It was even harder sleeping in the lumpy cot under the eaves with the memories she had now. Silas talking. Silas laughing. Holding her, making love to her. At night, she couldn't bear the thought of never seeing him again….

In the morning, she tried to be more rational. After breakfast—cornflakes and UHF milk—she coaxed an unsatisfying shower out of the rooftop cistern, still mud-warm from the previous day's heat, and washed her hair. She wouldn't miss the rudimentary plumbing, the dankness in the house in the evenings, the sense that things never *really* dried out, the spiders—and worse—in the corners of the woodshed, the huge production necessary to make a hot meal. She was tired of soup and sandwiches. She wanted to go to a good restaurant, be waited on. She longed to hear the electronic beep of the microwave when the timer went off. She even wanted to see something on television—anything!

The knock on the door just after nine was a surprise. Silas?

"Fanny! What are you doing here so early?" Eva had an ominous feeling when she saw the girl and dog. Fanny was dressed in long pants and a hooded cotton shirt and even had shoes on. She was out of breath. A bulging pillowcase slumped on the doorstep beside her.

"I've comed to stay with you, Eva," the girl announced solemnly, her eyes huge.

"'Come,'" Eva muttered automatically. "I've *come*—"

"I made up my mind. I bringed all my stuff, it's in here." She kicked the pillowcase. "I want to go home with you. You're a teacher. You could put me in your school. Sue Ellen and Monica are already in fourth grade. My dad won't let me go to a real school and if I don't get started, I'll *never* get to fourth grade!'' Fanny burst into tears.

''Oh, honey!'' Eva knelt down and gathered the child into her arms. ''Where's your dad now?''

''He taked Ivor back home,'' the girl sobbed. ''As soon as he left in the b-big b-boat, I decided to run away. I'm mad at my daddy. I came right over here when Auntie Aggie went out to get something in the g-garden. I think it was a r-radish!''

Bruno whined miserably. He sat down, stood up, then sat down again. Poor dog! Poor kid!

''Well, you come inside with me, honey, and we'll have some hot chocolate and talk this over. Does that sound like a good idea?''

''Y-yes,'' she gulped, then frowned. ''Hot chocolate with marshmallows?''

''Of course.'' Eva let go of the little girl and held the door open wider. ''Come inside?''

''Okay,'' Fanny said. She sighed dramatically and half carried, half dragged the pillowcase into the kitchen. Bruno padded in behind her, looking mournful. ''I wanted to leave Dad a note, 'cause that's what they do in books, but I can't even write!''

''Of course you can't, Fanny. You'd just be in

kindergarten if you were in a real school and the kindergarten kids can't read or write yet.''

''They can't?'' Fanny glanced up. Eva could see the news had cheered her. Either that or the prospect of hot chocolate.

''Gosh, no. They're just learning their letters and numbers and I'll bet you already know your letters and numbers.''

''You mean my A-B-C's? I do. My dad taught me all that.'' She nodded vigorously, her curls bouncing. ''And what's on the clock and how to play croquet, too.''

''See? Most kindergarten kids in real school don't even know what croquet is.'' ''What's on the clock,'' Eva realized, must be Fanny's version of how to tell time.

''I could show them. If my dad would let me go to school.'' Fanny surveyed the kitchen, her eyes lighting on the refrigerator. ''Hey! I wonder if there's any pop in your fridge yet? Can I look?''

''Sure. Why don't you go ahead and look.''

Fanny tiptoed over to the ancient fridge as though intending to ambush it and swung on the old-fashioned lever to open the door. ''Hey, there *is!*'' She emerged with a can of lemon-lime soda in her hand and a radiant smile. Eva had laid in a stock of soft drinks, as well as marshmallows and hot dogs for a possible beach picnic when her father and the girls returned.

"Would you like that?" Considering the situation, even Silas couldn't object to giving the child a can of pop.

"Yes, please! I like *pop!*"

Fanny sat at Eva's table, kicking her legs and sipping at the soda, which she wanted to drink out of the can, refusing Eva's offer of a glass. She'd apparently lost interest in the hot chocolate. Just as well. Eva didn't feel like firing up the wood cookstove just to warm some milk.

Consternation forgotten, Bruno lolled on the mat in front of the door, panting sociably, his warm brown gaze fixed approvingly on the girl. Fanny's tears had dried and she was her usual chatty self again.

Forgotten as well, Eva sincerely hoped, were her plans to run away and go to school.

FANNY WAS well prepared for her new life. Before Eva could convince the girl to walk back home with her, Fanny turned her pillowcase out onto the linoleum to show her what she'd packed. Two swimsuits, five or six stuffed toys, including the ladybug Eva had given her, her new sun hat, two pairs of shorts—although no shirts or socks or shoes—a battered box containing a game of Snakes and Ladders, and the red dress, inside out, she'd worn at the barbecue ten days ago. For Bruno she had a chew toy shaped like a rolled-up newspaper with the headline ''Man Bites Dog'' and a third of a box of jumbo Milk Bones. She'd also included three juice boxes and a package of raisins.

It was a good thing Fanny had stopped in before beginning her big adventure, Eva thought, helping the girl repack her pillowcase. Eva carried it over her shoulder while Fanny, singing at the top of her lungs, skipped ahead of her on the path through the woods. She didn't look as though she minded the interruption to her plans. Eva intended to talk to Silas as soon as possible. The school issue was just an indication of a deeper need, in her view. Silas needed to know how desperately his daughter wanted a more normal life than he could offer on Liberty Island.

Eva decided to mention her concerns to Mrs. Klassen.

She found her in the kitchen, snipping the ends off a colander full of green beans. ''Oh, Eva! I didn't know you were here.''

Eva told her about the early-morning visit. The housekeeper was astonished. She wiped her hands on her apron and her blue eyes filled with tears. ''Oh, my goodness. Running away! If anything ever happened to that child—'' She put one hand on her ample breast and raised her eyes to the ceiling. ''My heavens! Silas would—''

''Sit down, Agnes,'' Eva said, alarmed at the housekeeper's reaction. ''Nothing happened. And nothing *would* have happened anyway. Where could she go? This is an island. She can't get off.'' Which wasn't strictly true. Eva could see a determined Fanny doing something crazy, like pushing off in an abandoned rowboat with Bruno, a sort of child's version of *Robinson Crusoe.* Fortunately, all the boats on Liberty Island were well secured.

''I guess you're right,'' Mrs. Klassen said slowly, sinking into her rocking chair by the window.

''I just thought you should know. I'm going to talk to Silas about it, too.'' Eva spotted the teakettle simmering on the propane stove. ''Fanny's fine now. I brought her home and she ran off to see Matthew in the orchard. I have something I'd like to discuss, though. Shall we have some tea?''

''Tea sounds like a very good idea.'' Mrs. Klassen peered out the window. ''There are fresh cookies in that tin, dear. Put a few on a plate. You're *sure* she's all right now?''

''Of course she is. Fanny and that dog roam all over the island all the time. I don't suppose today is any different really, is it? Just the running away notion. I guess that's new.''

The housekeeper shook her head and twisted the

corner of her apron into a knot. ''She's a wild child! I've *never* approved of that girl running free as she does—'' she shook her head ''—but there's no telling her father anything!''

Eva poured the tea into two mugs, stirred some milk into both, and brought the plate of cookies to the table. ''Thank you, dear.'' The housekeeper glanced up as Eva handed her a cup. ''I don't suppose you could try convincing him? He seems to pay attention to what you have to say.''

''He does?'' Eva hadn't noticed that. It made her wonder what else the Klassens might have noticed about her relationship with their employer. ''Maybe it's just because I'm a teacher and I'm supposed to know a few things about children.''

''Maybe.'' Mrs. Klassen took a sip of her tea. ''What did you want to discuss, dear?''

Eva decided to jump right in. ''Silas told me about Fanny and her mother and everything, and...well, some of the reasons he wants to stay here year-round.''

The housekeeper stared at her. ''He's *told* you?''

Eva nodded. She didn't want to go into details about exactly *what* Silas had told her, in case the Klassens weren't aware of all the circumstances. ''I was wondering, Agnes, what you thought of—of all this? How did you and Matthew get involved?''

Mrs. Klassen sighed and was silent for a few moments. "I suppose you could say it really goes back to Ivor. And Silas's parents. His father ran off to the South Pacific with some woman years ago, did he tell you?"

Eva shook her head, carefully sipping her tea. She felt guilty, quizzing the elderly housekeeper like this, but she told herself it was justified. She had Fanny's best interests at heart. She needed to know as much as possible before she talked to Silas.

"We worked for them for many years. Oh, they are *such* a messed-up family! Greta—that's Silas's mother—is a lovely woman, mind you. She lives in Vancouver and she rarely comes here. She's—she's *European,* if you know what I mean. She was a Lord, too, in a way."

"A cousin?"

"No. Arden—Silas's father—married his stepsister. They weren't related at all, of course. The old man, Silas's grandfather, was married twice and his second wife, Birgit, had a daughter already. That was Greta, Silas's mother." Mrs. Klassen took a deep breath. "I don't know why I'm telling you all this, but it's just so *good* to talk to somebody about it besides Matthew. He's all right to talk to," she added loyally, "but he never talks back much."

Eva smiled and reached for a cookie. "Silas is an only child then?"

"Yes. He's the same age as my Ivor. Matthew

and I came to work for Silas's parents when Ivor was just a wee thing, three years old. The two boys grew up together. They were inseparable until—until the accident. In many ways, I was as much a mother to Silas as I was to my own boy.'' She gazed out the window for a minute or so, then fished a handkerchief out of her sleeve and wiped her eyes. She blew her nose loudly before stuffing it back up her sleeve. ''You see, after what happened to our son, how could we say no to Silas when…when little Fanny came along?''

She looked at Eva, her eyes red-rimmed and watery, then shook her head. ''I can't explain it. It's just that we knew, Matthew and I, what it was to have a damaged child, damaged through no fault of his own. But no matter how it happened—don't you see?'' She gave Eva a pitiful look. ''He'd never be the same again. His life would be different altogether. He's our boy but he's—he's not our boy.''

Eva felt sorry for the older woman. She'd given half her working life to serving the Lords and her job wasn't finished yet. It wouldn't be over until Silas faced up to what he'd done. And risk losing Fanny? The thought was ice in Eva's veins. *It would kill him.*

''Not that Fanny's damaged, you understand. Not at all. But she has no mother, poor little thing, and Silas was desperate. He doesn't know what else to do but keep her here on the island and I can't help thinking that's no life for a child...."

"So he asked you to come and help take care of Fanny?" she urged gently. "When he got her?"

"Yes. That's how it was. He needed us. He'd done so much for us over the years, helped us with all the therapy for Ivor, even helped us buy our cottage because we had so little put away with Ivor's expenses. I felt sure that it would only be for a short while, until Silas could see his way out of it, until things worked out somehow. Perhaps this Vivian—we never knew her, Matthew or I—would make things right. She cast a hopeful glance in Eva's direction. "Perhaps make arrangements to share custody or something, with Silas being the girl's natural father, y'see. Or perhaps they'd get married." Eva tried to maintain an encouraging expression. "He simply couldn't bear to be parted from the child, not after he knew she was his."

Mrs. Klassen sat in her chair, not rocking, gazing out the window for a few moments. The light was clear and sharp on her profile, button nose, round cheeks, pursed lips. Then she turned to Eva with a short laugh. "You know, dear, I don't think it really matters now. I really don't. Even if she wasn't really his, in the ordinary flesh and blood way, she's still his. They've had three years together. He's her father now. He could never be anything but."

Eva felt a sinking in her bones. The housekeeper was exactly right. It was all very well for Eva to think she could do something. But she couldn't. *There was no way out of this.*

Mrs. Klassen sighed. "Sometimes I dream of us back in our cottage in Hopkins Landing, Matthew and I. Retired, just tending our garden, having our boy over for dinner every Friday like we used to before Fanny arrived. Isn't it silly?" The housekeeper made an attempt at laughter and wiped at her cheeks with the apron corner. "I still call him a boy but he's the same age as Silas, just six months older." She shook her head and then stared out the window for a few more minutes, beginning to rock gently again.

"Until this business is settled somehow—" Mrs. Klassen's voice cracked and she turned to look beseechingly at Eva "—I don't know what else we can do."

CHAPTER TWENTY

SILAS DROVE Ivor back to the house he shared with five other physically and mentally challenged men, along with a live-in caregiver. At twelve, Ivor had suffered a broken neck and serious brain damage from being submerged in the water after a foolhardy dive from the rocks at Garden Bay, a favorite spot for kids to show off. Showing off had nearly cost Ivor Klassen his life.

It had cost Silas his best friend. Last night, as they'd sat out under the trees until the sun went down, Silas had reflected again on what might have been. Ivor had been enchanted with Fanny's latest trick, which was turning somersaults, and he'd clapped softly in his chair on the lawn, calling out her name repeatedly. Fanny, of course, had accepted the applause with her usual enthusiasm and had somersaulted over and over until she sprawled on the grass, laughing hysterically and too dizzy to stand.

"Fan-*ny*. Fan-*ny*. Fan-*ny*."

Silas had thought at the time: this is my family.

These are the people I love. A brain-damaged man. The found daughter, discarded by her own mother. An old couple, so true and simple that it made your heart hurt when you thought of all the people in the world who weren't. All that was missing from the tableau in front of him was the presence of the woman he didn't dare love….

Eva had seemed subdued last evening when he ferried her over from the mainland. Tired, she said. He hoped she wasn't having second thoughts about him. Was it only a week since he'd gone to her house in the storm? It seemed, in some ways, like a lifetime.

"Home," Ivor said as they drove along the street where he lived. "Home." Silas glanced at him. Until Ivor's accident, he and Silas been inseparable. Afterward, they had little in common. Ivor had spent years at the G. F. Strong Hospital in Vancouver, undergoing rehabilitation. To all appearances he looked fairly normal now, was able to walk and talk, but nothing was the same. Silas didn't think they even shared their boyhood memories anymore. Ivor rarely spoke, and, when he did, he never mentioned anything from the past.

Silas accompanied Ivor into the house with its clean, functional furniture and overbright fluorescent fixtures. As always, he hugged an unresponsive Ivor goodbye. Ivor never looked back, Silas had noticed over the years. He simply plodded directly into the television lounge to get on with...well, his life.

Matthew and Aggie needed to get on with their lives, too. It wasn't right that they should be stuck on Liberty Island because he was afraid to hire someone new, someone who might recognize Fanny from some old "lost child" poster. He'd never dreamed the situation on Liberty Island would go on as long as it had. Taking Fanny had been an impulse. There'd been no plan. At the time, Silas had looked forward to perhaps a year on the island, getting to know his daughter. That should be enough time for publicity about the kidnapping, if there was any, to die down. Then? Well, he'd hoped that by then Scott would have figured something out....

So here he was, stuck, too. His life on hold. Sometimes he felt like just turning himself in and accepting the consequences. Scott told him that would mean a jail sentence. He could face jail, but he couldn't face what that might do to Fanny, so the impulse to surrender was strangled as soon as it was born. She'd be sent to a foster family. He might lose her in the system before he got out of jail. Yes, there was a birth certificate—Scott had managed to check into that without drawing any attention to Silas—but there was no father named. And Vivian's address had been the rooming house where she'd lived for two weeks before she'd had the baby and six months afterward—before she'd decided to dump Fanny and go back to her husband in Washington. If it came down to it, since Vivian was married at the time of Fanny's birth, that bastard who hadn't wanted Fanny was probably considered by the law to be her father!

Even if Silas had a proper birth certificate showing he was Fanny's father, he was still guilty of kidnapping. The law was severe with people who abducted children, even their own.

Silas hadn't particularly minded his self-imposed seclusion on Liberty Island until Eva had arrived. What had started out as a mystery had become brilliantly clear to Silas over the past week. He was in love.

But what could he do about it? Could he marry Eva? Take her away from the island? No. His life was a mess. He didn't see any way out. Nor did Scott, and Scott had been working on extricating Silas from his difficulties since he'd found out that Fanny existed. First, how to gain access. Then, how to avoid going to jail. There were very few options: turn himself in, find Vivian again and work something out with her, or go to Sweden and start over.

Run away. That was the truth of it. Silas hated the thought of running away again.

He stopped at the lights where the coastal highway intersected Cowrie Street. Normally, he'd go straight through Sechelt but today he was going to the mall to pick up an order of groceries Aggie had phoned in to Clayton's IGA.

Which meant he'd be going right by the lane that led to Seaview Lodge.

What the hell. It was one o'clock. Lunch would be over. The old bird might be taking a nap soon. He stopped at the greengrocer's at the corner and picked up some flowers. Roses, freesias, daisies.

"These are for Mrs. Bonhomme," he said to the receptionist, holding up the bouquet. "She's in room—?"

"Room 127," came the cheerful reply.

Nothing to it, Silas thought as he strode down the hall. If Silas Lord Creations ever went belly up, he could get work as a delivery boy.

He knocked softly on the closed door.

"Yes?" He heard a quavery voice. "Come in."

Silas took a deep breath and turned the knob.

"Oh!" The old woman looked up, surprised. She was sitting on a neatly made bed, surrounded by letters and clippings. She'd obviously been sorting through papers. Tinny music emanated from the music box, which sat on the table in front of the window, the lid open. Silas recognized the rosewood box as the one Eva had shown him. "I wasn't expecting...ah." She paused, her eyes focused on the flowers. "Are those for *me?*"

"They are." Silas bowed slightly. He handed them to her and she gazed at the blooms with an odd expression. He noted that she was wearing the garnet necklace.

"Thank you," she said simply. "Would you mind fetching me that vase on the shelf over there?"

Silas got the vase and watched as she filled it with water from a glass jug on the bedside cabinet, probably her drinking water, then thrust in the flowers.

"There's no card. I wonder who they're from," she mused, patting the blooms lightly, rearranging them. Then she glanced up and frowned. "Oh—you're still here? You may go now, young man."

"They're from me." Silas remained where he was.

"You! Do I know you?" she asked imperiously, her eyes narrowing as she studied his face.

"I'm Silas Lord."

She put a hand on her throat and stared at him. Then she reached over to the music box and shut the lid abruptly, silencing the music. "You are—Hector's boy?"

"I'm his grandson, yes."

Her eyes fastened on his left wrist. "That watch—that belonged to Hector. Wh-what are you doing here?" Her lips trembled. She looked frightened and Silas felt a sudden wave of compassion for the old woman, so frail, so stubborn, so desperate to cling to the only thing she knew—the past.

"I thought we should meet. I intend to marry Eva—" Silas astonished himself as much as he astonished Doris Bonhomme "—which would make us related. It's time to end this ridiculous feud between your family and mine. No one cares anymore."

"I care!"

"Yes, you care. But it's time you forgot about it. The past is over."

"Is it?" she asked suddenly, her voice very low. "Is it *ever* over?" She gestured toward the chair that was positioned near the bed, in the window alcove, and Silas sat down. She picked up several letters from her bed and gave them to him. "Here."

Silas unfolded one of the letters. It was written in a spidery hand that seemed vaguely familiar. "Dearest Binchy," he read. He looked up. *"Binchy?"*

"That's me. He always called me that," she said, smiling. Silas was astonished at the change in her. A few minutes ago, he'd thought she might chase him bodily out of the lodge, laying about his shoulders with her cane as he went. Now she wore a soft expression. She seemed pleased with herself.

He skimmed through the pages, more out of politeness than curiosity. None of it—flowery love phrases, pet names, references to events he knew nothing about—made any sense to him. He was embarrassed. These were old love letters....

She suddenly banged her cane on the floor. "Do you promise to marry Eva?"

"I do. If she'll have me." Silas didn't know how he was going to convince Eva, but everything he'd said was true: he intended to marry Eva Haines.

"Do you love her—with *all* your heart?" the old lady cried. "Answer me!"

Silas nodded. "With all my heart." He handed the letters back but she wouldn't take them.

"Read them! See who they're from!" The old lady became very agitated, pushing several more of the yellowed, folded letters toward him.

Humoring her, Silas leafed through to the last page of the letter in his hand and held it to the light.

With all my heart, Hector.

Silas reached for several more letters. They were all from his grandfather to his "darling Binchy"—Doris Bonhomme.

EVA SPENT a pleasant afternoon at the rocks that guarded the entrance to Doris's harbor, making rubbings of the Indian petroglyphs. It took a bit of practice to get the technique right and she was glad she'd brought plenty of paper. When she was finished, she had several to give her father on his return trip, plus four more that she thought she would frame and hang in her apartment.

Was there any mail for her? She'd forgotten to ask Jack if he'd received anything from the school districts to which she'd sent applications. She'd used his return address so he'd be able to forward them to her at the Half Moon Bay Store general delivery, or at least phone her with the news, good or bad.

What would she do if she *didn't* get a full-time position? Eva hadn't really considered that possibility. Surely there was a job for her somewhere in British Columbia, even if it was in the far north or the deepest part of the Interior. A mining town. Cattle country. Well, if she had to do substitute teaching for another year, she would. At least then she wouldn't have to move.

Just thinking about going back to her cramped little apartment, throwing open the windows to air it out with stale city air, listening to the rumble of nonstop traffic, gave her a bruised feeling. It was so quiet and peaceful here on Liberty Island. It would seem strange to go to sleep each night with the lights of the passing traffic swirling over her ceiling.

Alone.

That was it—alone. Her talk with Mrs. Klassen had convinced her that taking the sensible course wasn't going to be as easy as she'd thought. Insist that Silas send Fanny to school. Persuade him that she needed playmates her own age. Argue for the Klassens' return to their little cottage, to be near their son.

The corollary kept rearing its ugly head: send Silas to jail for what he'd done. Tear him away from his daughter. Put Fanny in foster care.

Eva hadn't seen Silas since he'd brought her back last evening. She wondered how the family get-together had gone. Last night had been a catch-up visit, Mrs. Klassen had said this morning. Too much change upset her son, thus the invitation she'd extended for Eva to join them again on the coming Friday. This would be a return to the regular every-second-week dinner, which had been marked on Ivor's calendar since Christmas.

Eva wasn't sure she'd even be on Liberty Island next Friday.

When she got back to shore in the *Edie B.*, Andy was waiting for her. She rubbed his nose vigorously and scratched him under the jaw. The old donkey closed his eyes and grunted. Silly old thing! She could understand how Doris had become so attached to him.

There was a note on her door, a square of white paper pushed through with a thumbtack to secure it. Another invitation from Fanny? Her heart jumped when she realized it was from Silas.

But it *was* an invitation, handwritten. Place: The

Baths. Time: 6:00 a.m. tomorrow. Who: you and me. Dress: optional.

Eva smiled and closed her eyes, registering every single emotion that swept through her.

She'd be there.

CHAPTER TWENTY-ONE

THE HEAT OF THE SUN was just beginning to lift overnight moisture, like puffs of smoke, from the salal bushes and trees that lined the trail when Eva set off for The Baths the next morning. She'd awakened at sunrise, too early to meet Silas, and had lain in bed for half an hour, wondering what he was up to and what this day might bring. And where were Jack and the girls? How like her father not to inform her he'd been delayed or had changed his plans. Perhaps he wasn't stopping here on his way back from Desolation Sound, after all. It would be nice to know, but after all these years, nothing about her father's behavior surprised her.

A raven squawked as she approached the fork in the path, keeping to the left, to the track that emerged below the cabana, between the second and third pools. Eva wondered if this was the "big black bird" Fanny called George. She'd mentioned when they'd first met in Doris's kitchen that she had a bird and a squirrel for "friends," along with Bruno, of course. Poor kid.

Weren't ravens harbingers of bad news? Death, even? Or was that just Edgar Allen Poe material? Ravens were also important birds to the coastal Indian tribes that had once inhabited this area. A raven, the trickster, was central to the creation myth of the Haida, a group that lived farther north, in the Queen Charlotte Islands.

Eva wore only a towel and her flip-flops. Silas had said "dress optional" and she was taking him at his word.

She was ten minutes early, but Silas was waiting for her, leaning against one of the sandstone ledges that lined the third pool. He, too, wore a towel. A towel and a smile. He came toward her, looking up as she negotiated the shallow stone steps that led down to the pool of water, which appeared very dark and still this morning in the sharp-angled shafts of sunlight that penetrated the trees. Eva noticed he carried a small satchel, slung over one bare shoulder.

Eva had told Doris that Silas was about six feet tall or just over and pleasant looking. He was about that height, but he was a great deal more than "pleasant looking." Striking, maybe? Handsome, certainly. He was in desperate need of a haircut, but other than that, Silas Lord was a fine looking man. Hardly the pirate of her fantasies, but something much better. A kind, intelligent, sensitive man who was sexier in reality than she could ever have dreamed. Broad-chested, but lean at the same time, tanned, with broad shoulders and narrow hips, not an ounce of superfluous flesh, a flat, hard belly and straight, well-shaped legs. The shaggy undisciplined morning hair made him seem even wilder, even more appealing. Nothing but a towel and a satchel—and a smile—suited him perfectly, in her opinion. Especially here, in this remote island setting of rocks, water, trees and tangled undergrowth.

"Eva!" He put his arms around her and gazed into her eyes for a few stomach-fluttering seconds. Then he bent his head and kissed her.

His skin was cool and dry, his mouth warm and welcoming. Eva kissed him back, eager to touch him, impatient to reignite the passion they'd shared so many times in the past week.

What could be better? They were alone, with no one to disturb them except possibly the raven that had flown up into the hemlock tree. They hadn't seen each other for a day and a half and, Eva recognized with each second that passed, they *wanted* each other desperately....

"Oh, baby," Silas muttered, drawing back. He touched her lower lip with his thumb. His eyes were hot. "I missed you so much," he whispered. His voice sent shivers through her. Eva wasn't sure why he'd closed his hand over hers when she'd reached for the knot in his towel, stopping her. She wanted to tear their towels off and make love right here, leaning against the rocks, her arms twined around his neck, her legs wrapped around his waist, nothing but their crumpled-up towels offering protection against the rough sandstone.

"I didn't bring you here to make love to you," Silas began, breaking the kiss. Then he grinned. "Well, I did—but not right away. I've got a plan...."

"What's your plan?" she managed to ask, her breath coming in shallow gasps. Where was all her resolve of yesterday? To have a serious talk with Silas about his daughter and the Klassens? Her skin felt shockingly hot even though the morning air was cool, even chilly. Her breasts felt tight, compressed by the beach towel, which she'd wrapped snugly and modestly under her arms for the walk through the woods. Why? She could have run through the woods completely naked, a sort of Lady Godiva accompanied by a donkey instead of a horse, and no one would've seen her but the raven. Why hadn't she?

Habit. And reserve. She'd spent most of her life being careful. Eva had a sudden desire now to reverse that. Be free. Unfettered. Rid of clothes, of responsibilities, of good sense—

"Come here." Silas led the way to the pool. "I'll show you." The tide was high and Eva could see the pale ledge of the sandstone border angling for several feet under the water, bone-white against the green, secret depths.

Silas pulled at the knot that secured her towel and unfastened it, his eyes full on hers. The cloth fell away and Eva gasped slightly at the sensation of fresh air on overheated skin. She shook her head, untangling the hair on her shoulders and stood straight and proud before him.

"You now," she whispered, reaching for his towel. Silas was oddly restrained, as though this was some kind of ceremony. A dawn performance for two, with only a raven for a witness.

"Not yet." Silas unslung the canvas pack he carried and opened the top, not taking his eyes from her. He rummaged around and brought out something bright, something Eva couldn't immediately identify.

Then she realized it was a silver necklace. The piece he'd said he'd show her sometime—when everything was perfect?

"This is for you," he said, his voice rough. "Because I love you."

Eva held her breath, tears blurring her vision as she held his gaze. He'd never said anything about love before.... "I love you, too, Silas," she whispered, knowing it was right that she give words to what had been in her heart almost since she'd met him.

He put the necklace around her neck. It was an odd piece, with a curved band of silver that was open in the front, with two large stones—amber?—in the coils of silver at the ends of the partly open circle. The stones fit snugly in the hollows of her collarbone. There was a silver chain joining the open front, which Silas fastened. "This is so it doesn't fall off in the water."

"We—we're going swimming?" Eva's teeth were chattering, as much from the emotion that chased through her body as from the chill.

"Ever since I first saw you here when I was up there—" he pointed to the rocks, near the hemlock tree "—I have dreamed of seeing you wearing nothing but this." He put his thumbs on each stone in the necklace. "You were the most beautiful woman I had ever seen then and you are the most beautiful woman I have ever seen now. I want to share my life with you."

"Oh, Silas!" Eva reached up to pull him closer. At the same time she noticed that he'd let the knot in his towel slip. He put his arms around her and held her close, skin to skin. He kissed her until she couldn't stand it anymore. All she wanted was to lie down there, on the rocks or the nearby grass and make love….

"Oh!" She threw her arms around his neck as he

swept her up suddenly and took a step toward the water. *"No!"*

"Relax." He smiled. "I'm not going to throw you in. I'm going to do this slowly." He waded in. With the tide high, he could remain on the ledge until the water was nearly at his waist.

"That's too cold!" Eva said, grimacing as the water lapped up over her back.

"You can't deny me my greatest fantasy," he said, grinning.

"Which is...?" She clung tighter as he bent his knees, dipping her farther in.

"To see you swimming naked in this pool, wearing only this silver and amber necklace," he said. His eyes were dark. "The way I saw you the first time. You were like a mermaid. A sea-woman. With me beside you this time. With me telling you how much I love you. With me asking you to marry me, despite all the reasons you shouldn't. Despite all the reasons you should run as far and as fast as you possibly can from me, away from Liberty Island—do you understand what I'm saying?"

Eva held his gaze as long as she could. *Marry him?* Her heart was pounding.

"I love you, Eva," he repeated. "Will you marry me?"

She nodded. "I will, Silas. I'll marry you."

"Forever and ever, no matter what?"

"Forever and ever."

He kissed her and then, still linked, he stepped off the ledge and they sank into the pool.

"Hey!" She heard the raven squawk as she broke their kiss and yelled. That water was cold! Silas laughed, treading water, his hands resting lightly on her waist. He kissed her again, then began to swim beside her, a sidestroke that let him watch her as she swam slowly to the other side of the pool.

Eva had never felt more desired. He'd asked her to *marry* him? She'd accepted! She'd been stunned, shocked—but, oddly, not surprised. So much had occurred in two weeks. Now this. What else could possibly happen?

She grabbed at the rocks on the other side of the pool to steady herself. Was she crying? Or was it just the salt water dripping from her face and hair?

"Eva!" Silas was in front of her, one hand on the rocks, the other reaching out for her. He put his arm around her. She shivered and clung to him, the cold, hard silver of the necklace biting into her throat.

He kissed her again. She closed her eyes and savored his touch, his taste, his presence. "Had enough?" he asked.

She nodded, her teeth chattering.

"Let's go back to the other side," he whispered. "I'll warm you up."

Eva turned and kicked out ahead of him. She was aware that he was right behind her. As her feet found the ledge, he pulled her against him again. "You're probably aware that it's pretty hard for guys to, uh, *do* anything in cold water like this."

Eva wiped the water from her face with both hands and smiled. "Really?"

"Yeah." He had a pained expression but his eyes were dancing. "Even if they really want to."

"Difficult but—" Eva paused as she wrapped her legs around Silas's hips and pulled his face toward her "—not impossible, right?"

"No," he breathed, adding between kisses, "not impossible."

"SO, WHAT *else* is in your plan?" Eva traced the muscles in Silas's chest with a blade of grass. She was sitting up, relishing the increasing warmth of the sun in the nest Silas had made for them in a clearing near The Baths. He'd even put down a quilt before meeting her. "Will we keep living here?" Somehow, she couldn't yet bring herself to say "after we're married." The whole concept was too fresh and new and...scary.

Silas lay out on his back in the sun, one arm under his head and his eyes shut. She'd known for some time that he was a nude bather and sunbather, obviously much more than she was, from the overall tan he'd acquired. There was something so elemental about the two of them out here in the sun, totally naked, totally natural.

He batted at the grass irritant as she tickled one nipple. "Would you live here with me?" He frowned slightly. "Knowing the circumstances?" Eva wasn't sure if his frown was because of her question or the annoying progress of the blade of grass.

"I would." Eva closed her eyes. It would be hard, but she was making a commitment to the man, not the place. Circumstances could change—

"Oh, baby." Silas's free hand was warm on her shoulder. She opened her eyes and stared into his. "I couldn't ask you to do that. I—I've thought things over during the past few days and I've come to a decision about Fanny and me and the Klassens, and now you."

"What's that?"

"I'm going to turn myself in."

"Oh, no, Silas!" Eva was shocked. She couldn't marry Silas only to lose him so soon....

"'For better or for worse,'" he quoted softly. "This would be the worst, Eva. But I promise that once this is behind me, our future is clear."

"What about Fanny?"

"Fanny was always my biggest concern. I'm taking a gamble. I think if we got married right away and I ended up having to go to jail—''

''Silas!''

He put his thumb over her mouth. ''Shh, honey. Face the facts. It's a very strong likelihood.''

''But you're her *father.* You were just trying to protect her. Who knows what would've happened to Fanny if you'd left her there.'' Eva couldn't believe she was now defending Silas for something that she'd always believed was wrong—kidnapping. ''Can't you *prove* it somehow? So you wouldn't have to go to jail?''

''Proof that I'm her father doesn't matter. I have proof. DNA, which is as iron-clad as you can get,'' Silas said grimly. ''But even if I'm Fanny's real father—and I am—and even if my name is on her birth certificate, which it isn't, I still can't abduct her from a public playground. It's against the law. You know that.''

Eva studied her own hands for a few seconds. Her nails were short, broken, her hands stained. She could use a manicure. ''When did you get the DNA testing done?'' The knowledge that he'd gone so far as to get scientific evidence of his paternity surprised her. As Mrs. Klassen had said, Eva knew, deep down, that regardless of what the DNA results would have been, positive or negative, Silas really was Fanny's father in every sense that mattered.

He'd raised her, he'd loved her, he'd taken care of her, spent time with her, protected her…would die for her.

"It was Scott's idea. My lawyer. Scott wanted proof for when the time comes, when I have to face a judge and jury." Silas stared at the blue sky high above the gently waving fronds of the cedar tree beside them. "He's a good friend. He thought maybe it would be useful information. I'm not sure what his strategy was then, but I didn't hesitate. I'd do anything that would help me make my case. I still would. But—" he stroked the curve of her cheek "—what about you? Your dreams, your goals."

"Teaching?"

"Yes."

"That can wait," Eva said firmly. "I haven't heard about any of the applications I made, so I might be substitute teaching this year anyway."

"I love you, Eva. I promise I'll make this up to you somehow."

"I love you, too, Silas. No matter what happens."

"What about getting married right away?"

"I suppose that would allow Fanny to stay with me, as her stepmother, if—if—" Eva could not bring herself to utter the possibility that Silas would go to jail.

He laughed. "Exactly. Do you have a problem

with that? I suppose you've always wanted a big wedding, two hundred guests, the right dress and all that girly stuff—''

''Do you care about what kind of wedding we have?''

''No.'' Silas laughed. ''I've always been more concerned with finding the right woman. And to think,'' he said, his eyes on hers, ''she found me.''

''Right now, a big wedding is the least of my concerns. Besides,'' Eva said, smiling, ''we could always have two.''

''Two weddings?''

''Why not? One now and one later.''

''When I get out of jail?''

''Please don't *say* that!''

Silas pulled her down and kissed her. Eva knew she was making the right decision, for all the right reasons, but something still niggled at the back of her mind.

''Silas?''

''Mmm?''

''How long have you had this—this plan, as you call it?''

He paused, as though reflecting on how to phrase his answer.

She rose up on her elbow and stared down at him, giving him her best stern-teacher look. ''The *truth,* Silas.''

"The truth," he repeated. "You really want the truth? It's not pretty, I'm ashamed to say."

"The truth." Eva heard the raven squawk again, somewhere in the distance, then the heavy sound of his wings flapping as he flew through the trees nearby. Good riddance!

"Okay. I first got the idea of marrying you when I found out you were an elementary teacher."

"What?" Eva gaped at him. She was prepared for some kind of crazy story from Silas, but not this.

"Think about it. I was wildly attracted to you already, had been ever since I'd first seen you here at The Baths. I was in an increasingly difficult situation with Fanny. She wanted to go to school, she wanted to have playmates—"

"All of which, by the way, I agree with."

"Right. Well, I saw you as the answer to my prayers. I'd marry you, if you'd have me, and you could take over Fanny's schooling as her stepmom and it would all work out."

"It would *not* all work out." Eva digested Silas's explanation. "That was underhanded, conniving, manipulative and—"

"And stupid," he finished for her. "Everything changed the night of the storm." He hesitated. "Maybe it was those goats. Maybe they interceded on my behalf."

"What goats? What are you talking about?"

"The storm. I could've sworn I heard hooves scraping on pebbles, like Andy walking around. When I yelled for him, he wasn't there and the next morning I found out you'd locked him in the shed."

"So there are goats on the island, after all." Eva liked to think that was true. After all, Doris's husband had wanted to be buried on Abel's Peak, with the mythical goats.

"Maybe. Anyway, that was when I realized I wasn't in control. I realized there wasn't any plan. I realized I was hopelessly in love with you and if I couldn't convince you to marry me, I didn't know what I'd do."

"But you did. And it turned out that I was in love with you, too." Eva smiled. "Happy endings all around." She felt a little hurt but at the same time, would she want a husband who wasn't totally honest with her? Besides, although he'd confessed his devious initial idea, she didn't have a shred of a doubt that he loved her now, goats or no goats.

And that, as he said, changed everything.

CHAPTER TWENTY-TWO

SILAS WOKE at dawn, which was his favorite time of day. He liked to think in the early mornings, before the rest of the world was up. He took his coffee to the long, room-length windows in the living room, a view overlooking the mountains and the harbor.

Sun washed the twin peaks of the Lions to the north, part of the range that contributed to Vancouver's well-deserved reputation as having one of the most spectacular settings in the world. To his left sprawled the gleaming vista of Coal Harbour, the Lions Gate Bridge and the sweep of English Bay with its usual contingent of freighters at anchor, awaiting their turn to come into the harbor. The forested headland marking the southern margin of the bay held the University of British Columbia.

There were worse cities in which to bring up a family. Fanny. Sisters and brothers one day. A normal family, with joys and frustrations, ups and downs, a house in the city somewhere—he was already thinking of getting rid of the condo—and a summer place on Liberty Island. A happy family, constructed out of the ruins of his own and the disappointments of Eva's. He'd be taking on a slightly mad father-in-law and a couple of sisters-in-law, one of whom hadn't been seen for three years.

Eva had accepted his proposal of marriage and that was all that mattered. He'd convinced her to move her clothes to his house, which made sense considering how little furniture remained at the Bonhomme place, not to mention no domestic comforts at all. At least the Lord house had decent plumbing and a generator. She'd set herself up in the guest bedroom there and they'd announced their plans to the household. Aggie had literally wept with joy and Fanny had been ecstatic, dancing all over the kitchen and hugging Bruno until he hid under the table. Even Matthew had grinned broadly and shaken Silas's hand half a dozen times.

If only all his ideas were as well received.

Then, on Monday, they'd had the once-in-a-lifetime experience of transporting an unwilling donkey in the open afterdeck of the *Windjammer* to the Half Moon Bay wharf. The retired army man and his spinster sister had collected him there, gushing over the seriously ticked-off beast, feeding him carrots and apples and enticing him into the van they'd rented for the trip to his new home at the Davis Bay Petting Zoo.

Silas was relieved to be finished with the operation, even though he had to deal with Fanny's tears when they got back. Her grief at losing Andy turned to happiness when he informed her that not only could they visit Andy anytime they wanted, but that the next day they were flying to Vancouver—Silas, Fanny and Eva—to have dinner with Grandma. And the day after that, Eva would take Fanny shopping for school clothes while Silas tended to some new client appointments at Silas Lord Creations.

The plan was that Eva and Fanny would meet him at noon and he'd take them for lunch at Cloud Nine at the top of the Landmark Hotel. The menu was immaterial; the view from the thirty-ninth floor revolving restaurant was the best in the city. He wanted Fanny to get a good look at her new home.

Silas cradled his mug in both hands. Was this the beginning of a new future for the three of them? He barely permitted himself to hope. Eva had convinced him it was possible. And what better city in which to blend in with his half-Haitian daughter than one where more than a million people spoke dozens of languages, came from dozens of countries and all kinds of ethnic backgrounds?

All he had to do was go to the law and confess his crime....

Silas took a deep breath and turned away from the window, draining his lukewarm coffee. He'd never been afraid of jail; he'd just been afraid of what it would do to Fanny. Silas hoped he could convince a judge that his daughter would be safe and happy with a stepmother who loved her. His nightmare was being forced to turn his daughter over to child protection services and a foster home. Surely that wouldn't happen now, with his marriage to Eva. Money, promises, guarantees, a jail term—Silas was willing to do whatever it took to put the past behind them and secure a future together.

He ran a hand over his shaggy head and glanced at the old Rolex on his wrist. Just past eight. He had two appointments this morning at Silas Lord Creations, one with a Japanese businessman and one with a couple from San Francisco. If he left within the half hour, he'd have time to stop at Lorenzo's, his favorite barbershop on Broughton, get a haircut and a shave, with Lorenzo's insider sports gossip thrown in for free. Time to leave the Liberty Island image behind and metamorphose into a solid city businessman, the kind of man who might be able to impress a family judge that he was competent and capable. Appearances weren't everything but, as he could hear Aggie say, it never hurt to look the part. Or as his uncle Leo might put it, why shoot a hole in your own goddamn foot when the whole world's lining up to do it for you?

Besides, he thought with a flood of remembered

pleasure that made him smile as he stepped into the shower, he was getting married as soon as it could be arranged. Maybe even this week. A city hall wedding now, and, as Eva said, they could do it all over again later if they wanted.

How could life be any more perfect than it was right now? Well, not going to jail would be nice. Towel around his waist, Silas strode into the adjoining dressing room and picked out a crew neck shirt and a light-gray linen summer suit. A tie? No, that was going too far.

Dressed, he went into the second bedroom to gaze at his daughter before leaving. She was asleep, her bed full of stuffed animals here as it always was on Liberty Island. Poor little girl, all tuckered out. She'd been so excited to come to Vancouver for the first time yesterday. Meeting Grandma last night at the restaurant had been another huge adventure. Greta had welcomed the child and her son's fiancée with open arms, as Silas had known she would.

The Newfoundland was in his usual place at the foot of her bed, where he'd returned after Silas had taken him for a dawn run along the seawall. He raised his massive head when Silas opened the door and slapped the carpet with his heavy tail, a slow thump-thump. The 170-pound animal hardly fit the profile of standard apartment pet, usually a toy poodle or a pug these days, but the concierge, a kind man, had pretended not to notice the big black dog.

Then Silas went to his bedroom to say goodbye to Eva. She was awake and stretched her arms toward him when he entered the room. "You up already?" she asked sleepily.

Silas bent down and kissed her soft mouth. It was tempting to get back into bed and take up where they'd left off. How he loved this woman! How lucky he'd been that she'd decided to come to Liberty Island this summer to pack up Doris's junk. Would he ever have met her otherwise? He hadn't related the extraordinary story Doris had told him yet, but he'd tell her soon. Maybe at their family dinner on Friday. The Klassens would be interested, too. "Early? It's almost half-past-eight."

"It is?" She half sat, leaning on her elbows, the sheet edging down to reveal the creamy tops of her breasts.

"Yes, it is, sleepyhead." He kissed her lightly, then tucked the sheet around her bare shoulders and stood up. "I'm heading to the office. Have fun with Fanny this morning. I'll see you two at lunch."

"Right. Your office?"

He nodded. She slid back down onto the pillow and yawned. "Fanny awake?"

"No. I think yesterday was a pretty big day for her."

"And today's going to be another big day. I'm really looking forward to it, Silas." Her eyes met his. She was so serious, yet so relaxed and happy at the same time. "I have a good feeling about today. I have a good feeling about—about everything."

He knew what she meant. He was hoping—as he knew she was, too—that somehow Scott would still be able to extricate him from this hellish situation. Silas wasn't as optimistic as she was, though.

"Bye, love." He kissed her again and left the room, closing the door gently behind him. He locked the apartment and pushed the button for the elevator.

Shave, haircut and then? Then the rest of his life.

"HI!" Tracy's desk, as usual, was clear and clean. "Mr. Suzuki had to cancel today, so I booked him for tomorrow morning. I hope that's okay?"

"Fine." He was planning to stay in Vancouver until Friday, returning with Fanny and Eva in time for the regular dinner with Ivor and the Klassens. Silas watched as his assistant unlocked and opened a lower desk drawer and took out a sheaf of papers and envelopes. He felt guilty; he hadn't gone through all the mail she'd given him last time.

"Here you go."

"Thanks." Silas idly flipped through it and frowned. "So, I'm clear until the other appointment? Eleven o'clock?'' He had work he could do. It was just before ten now.

''No. I called them and luckily they were able to come in early. They're very eager. Your reputation precedes you.''

''Sure it does,'' Silas said with a smile. ''If you only knew, Tracy. By the way, did I tell you I'm getting married?''

''Silas!'' He was pleased that he'd actually managed to upset his unflappable assistant's equilibrium. ''Who's the lucky gal?''

''Eva's her name. You don't know her. She's meeting me here for lunch. She and a, uh, little girl.'' Silas hadn't informed Tracy of all the reasons he was spending most of his life on Liberty Island. Scott's advice had been to keep things quiet. Tracy knew he had a studio there, a family place, and that he liked the peace and quiet. She didn't ask questions.

''Well!'' His assistant beamed. ''I can't wait to meet her. The Campbells are already here. I asked them to wait in the studio—I hope that was all right?''

Silas stood and stuffed the unopened mail into the microfiber sack Tracy handed him. ''Fine. Did they say what they're interested in?''

''No. But I thought they'd enjoy a chance to look

at some of your pieces while they waited. They seem very keen to meet you.''

Silas grimaced. Dealing with clients wasn't his favorite part of the business. Clients often had ideas that didn't really suit them—in Silas's view—or had unreasonable ideas about how much custom work like his was going to cost. Perhaps one out of every three or four meetings resulted in a commission. Sometimes the client got cold feet. Often Silas turned down the project. He could afford to take only work that really interested him.

Silas picked up the sack of mail and strode toward the studio-cum-office he kept at the back of the shop, with big windows that overlooked Robson Street.

''Hello,'' he said as he opened the door. ''Mr. and Mrs. Campbell? Sorry I kept you waiting.''

A tall black man in a business suit stood at one of the brightly lit showcases that lined the wall of Silas's office. Next to him stood a black woman. Tall, graceful, beautifully dressed.

She turned as Silas closed the door behind him.

He felt like he'd been hit in the solar plexus by a cement truck.

''Vivian!''

CHAPTER TWENTY-THREE

VIVIAN WAS A WOMAN born to wear emeralds.

One of the most beautiful pieces he'd ever made, a coiled snake, a tiny stylized boa constrictor, made of twenty-two-carat white and yellow gold with a large emerald eye, had been a centerpiece of the photographic essay he'd done when he'd asked Vivian to model for him. It had been utterly gorgeous contrasted with the dark skin of her firmly muscled upper arm and had sold, several months later, for a huge sum to a sheik from Qatar. Silas had hoped the sheik's purchase had been given to a woman as suitable.

"*What are you doing here?*" Silas instantly regretted his outburst. But how could he have prevented it? He tossed the mail sack onto his desk and tried desperately to take in this shocking new situation.

"Silas, I know this is astonishing to you. I will explain." Her voice had haunted him for years. It was the same, better English but still accented with the intonations of her first language, French, tempered with a Caribbean lilt.

"How are you?" Silas took the initiative and extended his hand. "Mrs. Campbell, I presume." They were in his office, dammit, and if this was about his daughter, he intended to get some answers. Maybe LaPre had been a stage name.

"Yes." She smiled tentatively and her eyes darted to the other man. "And please to meet my husband, Armand."

Ah, delighted to finally meet the man I cuckolded—the man who wanted to abort my daughter....

Silas had to bite his tongue as he shook Vivian's husband's hand. *Manners, manners.* "How do you do, Mr. Campbell? Armand, is it? So, have you seen anything here that interests you?" He waved around the studio.

Maybe he'd just ignore Vivian and everything that had happened between them. After all, it was a long time ago. Maybe this really *was* about jewelry.... They certainly looked, both of them, as though they could afford it. Vivian had definitely moved up a step or two in the world. And there was no way she could possibly know that he had Fanny—or that he even knew about her.

"You have so many beautiful things here," Vivian began, one hand gracefully taking in the lighted showcases along the wall. "I—I knew you were an *artiste,* of course, but I did not realize you were so successful."

"I wasn't—then. You look as though life has been treating you kindly, Vivian." Silas turned to her husband. "I gather you're aware that your wife and I are acquainted."

"Yes," he responded bluntly. "That is why we are here." He gave Vivian a hard look.

"Oh?" Silas decided to feign ignorance. "You are not interested in commissioning a piece of jewelry, then. How unfortunate! I've always thought Vivian suited emeralds."

"Silas!" Vivian's voice was anguished and he was immediately sorry he'd stooped to sarcasm. She was the mother of his child; she deserved better.

"Didn't you receive my letter?" Her eyes were large and lustrous, so like Fanny's. "I wrote to you several times."

"You did?" Silas wished he'd opened all the letters in the last batch of mail Tracy had given him. Now that he thought of it, he recalled seeing an envelope postmarked San Francisco but he'd tossed it back in the pile with the rest. The name *Campbell* meant nothing to him. Summers were downtimes. Holidays. If he'd been desperate for work, he'd probably have opened all his mail. Otherwise, he operated on the basis that if something was really important, he'd hear about it eventually, much to the distress of Uncle Leo, who believed in being prepared for all contingencies.

Uncle Leo was right. If he'd received—and read—a letter from Vivian, he could likely have avoided this meeting.

"So, is this a visit then? Maybe you can you tell me what it's about. Please—" he gestured toward the sofa and upholstered chairs in the seating area "—sit down."

"I—I was afraid you wouldn't see me. That's why we made the appointment at your work." Vivian glanced nervously at her husband. He moved decisively to one of the chairs.

"My wife and I have only been married for eight months," Armand Campbell began. "She was formerly married to Gregory LaPre. She told me about her relationship with you." He stared at Silas and Silas stared back.

"I can't see that any relationship I may or may not have had with your wife before you married her is any of your concern," Silas began stiffly.

"Silas," Vivian interrupted. "Please." She held up both hands. "Please, Armand. Let me explain. Let me speak to Silas myself."

Her husband made an impatient gesture. "Go ahead." He got to his feet again, thrust his hands in his pockets and began studying Silas's showpieces.

"Silas," Vivian began again. "You must please forgive me. I have done some—some very bad things. I didn't tell you when I met you that I was married."

"Never mind that, Vivian," Silas said dismissively. "It's history. All's well that ends well. You're happily married now." He glanced toward the unforgiving back of Armand Campbell.

"That is true." Silas noticed that Armand threw his wife a private look. *A loving look.* "I was very unhappy then. I married Gregoire for a bad reason, in order to get into the United States from Haiti. A green card marriage, as they say. For immigration. I tried to love Gregoire, but it was ...*difficile.*" She shook her head sadly. "I left Gregoire and came to Vancouver with the Caribbean dance troop and I was very happy here for a while. I met you." She smiled shyly and Silas began to breathe a little easier. For some reason, she needed to get all this off her chest.

"Things seemed to be going easier for me. Then you left Vancouver and I—I discovered I was *enceinte,* Silas."

She must have expected more of a reaction. Silas remained stone-still, gazing at her. "I see."

"Yes. I was going to have a baby and I didn't know what to do. I couldn't stay with the troop, so I went back to my husband. He said he wanted to make a go of our marriage, but when he found out I was *enceinte,* he—he wanted me to get rid of it.''

Even though Silas knew all these details from the private investigator, it hurt hearing them from Vivian. *Why hadn't she told him?* ''Why didn't you contact me?'' he asked, his voice harsher than he'd meant it to be. ''I could've helped you.''

''I didn't know how to,'' she said simply. She twisted the wedding band on her left hand. Silas noted that it was matched with a sizable diamond. ''I was married to Gregoire and he said he would take me back and I believed him. Besides, the baby was an—an accident. I knew you were not interested in having a baby with me.''

''That's true.'' Hard as it was for Silas to say, he had to admit she'd been right. A baby at that time in his life? With a woman who'd modelled for him and with whom he'd had a passing affair? She was one among many at the time. Yes, he'd have wanted to run as fast and as far as he could....

''So I went back to my husband.'' She seemed relieved to know she hadn't misjudged Silas: he'd had no intention of marrying her, baby or not. He wasn't proud of himself, but it was the raw, unvarnished truth.

''Gregoire said I had to choose between him or the baby. He wanted me to get rid of the baby but I wouldn't. I took a boat to Victoria when the birth was close...." Her voice tumbled on. Silas could tell she'd been waiting to talk about this for a long, long time. "I thought I could manage on my own. But I—I couldn't. I had no money, no friends, no family. I had the baby, it was a little girl, and after a few months, I—I just couldn't handle it anymore...." Her voice trailed off. Her eyes were brimming with tears.

"What happened?" Silas knew what had happened; he had to hear Vivian say it.

"I—I had met some people there. They were kind and they had several children of their own, plus they were looking after children for some other people so I—I left my baby with them. I thought I would go back later, maybe after I had convinced Gregoire to accept the baby and—" She began to weep softly and stopped to take a tissue out of her purse. Silas's nerves were screaming. She had admitted Fanny was his child—why hadn't she put his name on the birth certificate? And she wasn't talking about turning Fanny over to child welfare—she was talking about a private foster family.

He turned to Vivian's husband. "Where do you fit into this?" He needed an outlet for the surge of violence he felt just under the surface of his own skin. Better to spar with Armand Campbell than his wife.

"I urged Vivian to tell you everything. I knew it

was eating her up inside and I didn't want my marriage poisoned by what had happened in the past.'' Armand Campbell walked to the big windows and looked down on Robson Street, ignoring Silas. ''That's it. Self-interest, pure and simple.''

Silas turned back to Vivian. ''Why didn't LaPre accept the baby?''

''Would you have?'' Her anguished eyes met his. ''Would *any* man?''

''I don't know,'' Silas said. ''You're probably right. I'd prefer to think I'd accept something like that if I loved a woman, but maybe I wouldn't.''

''You don't know until you have faced it!'' she exclaimed passionately. ''How do you think I felt to have to give up my baby? My husband would pay, oh, yes, he didn't mind that—he sent money every month to those people—but he would not permit me to keep my child! He did not want *any* children, not even his own!''

Silas was about to explode. Money! He got up and walked to his desk and back. The telephone. He needed to talk to Scott. Get him over here. The people she was talking about were so-called private foster parents. Predators. They had had nothing to do with the government or child services. No wonder there'd been no big publicity push to find Fanny after he'd abducted her. Perhaps the police had never been told. They'd taken money to keep Fanny, whose mother was a Haitian alien living in another country. They knew no one would turn them in. How long had they continued taking the money after Fanny had disappeared? It was all illegal—everything! He needed this documented. He needed a witness, someone besides Armand Campbell.

"So you decided I should know about it," he said heavily. "After all this time."

"Yes!" she cried. "I always felt bad about this. *Terrible.* After Gregoire and I separated and—and then we divorced, I managed to put my life back together. I met Armand. I decided to get my daughter back but—" She began to sob violently and her husband strode to her and took her in his arms.

"Don't cry, baby," Silas heard him mutter. "This is a good thing, baby. You know that. You need to get this out of your system. It's best this way," he soothed. He glared at Silas.

Silas almost felt as though he wasn't part of whatever was going on here. As though all of this was somehow his fault. And he was the father! He poured a glass of ice water from the carafe on his desk, then picked up the phone. "Tracy?" he said tersely. "Call Scott. Get him here immediately. *Now.*" He hung up, not waiting for her response.

"Who the hell were you talking to?" Armand Campbell demanded.

"My assistant."

"What for?"

"I want my lawyer here. I want him to take an affidavit—"

"What the hell for?" Campbell sounded outraged.

"I want a record of what Vivian is telling me now. After five—nearly six years. That I have a child. That I am the father of her baby. I want a birth certificate—"

"I didn't put your name as father," Vivian said, stifling her sobs. "I was married to Gregoire LaPre, what could I do? I put unknown. He didn't want me to put *his* name!" She began to cry again.

"It doesn't have my name on it," Silas retorted, "but by God, it *should* have my name on it! I want Vivian to swear that I'm the father—"

"You are pathetic, do you know that?" Armand Campbell's eyes glittered. "Pathetic! You seduce women and you bugger off to Europe and then you yell about rights. Don't you see how this is upsetting my wife?"

"It's upsetting *me*, dammit!" he shouted. "And I suppose *you've* never slept with a woman you haven't married."

"But *Silas!*" she wailed. "Don't you see? It doesn't matter anymore. That's what I told you in the letters. Why didn't you write? That's why we came here, to tell you—"

"*What* doesn't matter anymore?" Silas broke in. He could shake them both, Vivian and her new husband, knock their damn heads together.

Vivian burst into a fresh gale of tears and Armand turned to Silas. "The kid's gone. Disappeared. The people who were supposed to be looking after her say she was taken from a playground three years ago. Now they've disappeared, too. Moved." Vivian's husband held up his hands in a gesture of exasperation.

Silas stared at them both. Of course Fanny was gone. He'd taken her. But he wasn't telling them that. Not until he had every single detail Vivian had told him down on paper, signed and witnessed.

"Gone," he repeated blankly.

"I want my baby back!" Vivian wailed. "I want you to forgive me for the bad things I've done. I'm sorry, Silas. I'm so sorry! I want you to try to help me find her—we must *find* her!"

Dazed, Silas looked to Armand for help. What was she talking about? "Vivian is pregnant now," he said quietly. "I think that's what has brought this all on again. I support her in trying to find her daughter—"

"*My* daughter!"

"Yeah, yeah, your daughter," he repeated wearily, and Silas could see how hard this had been on him. Were they telling him they wanted Fanny *back?* ''I want her to go to the police—''

''No!'' Silas paced back and forth in front of the windows. He needed to think. He needed Scott to get here, damn him! Where *was* he? He needed—''Excuse me for a minute, will you?''

He stepped to the outer door and gestured to Tracy. ''Is Scott on his way?''

''Yes. He said he'd get here as soon as he could. What's this about?''

''Good.'' Silas ignored her question. ''Now, will you please call my fiancée.'' He gave her Eva's cell phone number. ''Tell her to take a cab to Cloud Nine. She is not to come here under any circumstances. Understand? I'll meet her at noon.'' He glanced at his watch. It was already after eleven. ''Better tell her I may be late.''

''Silas! What in the name of heaven is going on?''

But Silas had already shut the door.

EVA TIPPED THE CAB driver and then gathered up all their bags. They'd bought more for Fanny in an hour and a half than Eva had bought for herself in the past six months.

''Can I carry my new shoes?'' Fanny stood proudly on the sidewalk, waiting for Eva to extricate herself from the vehicle.

"Of course. Here you go." Eva handed her the bag. "You're sure a good shopper."

"I am?"

"You've worn me out already." She meant it. They'd been through the children's department at The Bay like a whirlwind, had bought a jacket, shoes, one skirt, three tops, two pairs of pants and two pairs of pajamas and they weren't finished yet. Tomorrow morning they both had hair appointments at Suki's on South Granville.

"You're funny!" Fanny swung the shopping bag with the shoes in it. "I'm not tired at all." She pointed at the art deco building beside them. "Is this where my daddy works?"

"When he's in Vancouver." Eva walked to the entrance of the building and smiled her thanks as a tall, harried-looking man held the door for them, then hurried through himself. They were a little early. Since they had the time, though, she wished they'd taken a cab back to the condo to get rid of the shopping bags before meeting Silas. Still, she couldn't deny Fanny the thrill of showing her father all her new purchases.

The man who'd held the door for them was waiting at the elevator. He jabbed at the button several times, then strode toward the stairs. Normally, Eva would also have walked up the two flights, but not dragging half of Fanny's new school wardrobe.

Fanny had been excited about shopping, but Eva knew the experience had been somewhat overwhelming. The girl had stared at everything, which made sense, since everything was new to her. She'd been fearful of the escalator in the department store but once she'd learned how to get on it, Eva couldn't get her off. Shopping was tiring enough, even more so when you were spending someone else's money, but keeping track of an irrepressible five-year-old at the same time was exhausting. Especially a five-year-old who talked to everyone and stopped on the street to admire pigeons.

"Can I push the button?"

Eva nodded. "Go ahead, Fanny." For all the good it would do....

They got off the elevator and to their right was a door with frosted glass proclaiming Silas Lord Creations with a button beside the door and a sign that read, "Please ring for admittance."

Eva pointed to the button and Fanny was more than happy to ring—and ring.

"That's enough, honey."

The door opened—and they were staring at the same man they'd seen downstairs.

"Hi, again," he said distractedly and turned to a slim, dark woman wearing a navy suit behind the reception desk. "Tracy? Shall I go in?"

"Yes," she said. "He's expecting you." She

smiled hesitantly at Eva and Fanny and walked around to the front of her desk. ‘‘Is there something I can help you with?’’

‘‘I’m Eva Haines,’’ Eva said. ‘‘I’m afraid we’re early. We’re here to meet Silas for lunch.’’

The woman paled. ‘‘Oh, my goodness—I’ve been trying to call you. Did you get my message?’’

‘‘Gosh, I don’t think my phone rang.’’ Eva frowned and set down her bags. Now, where was her cell? There it was, in the bottom of her purse, its low-battery light blinking weakly. ‘‘I didn’t hear it ring. Is—is something wrong?’’ Her heart sank. Had something happened to Silas?

The receptionist was definitely rattled. ‘‘Oh, no. Just—just have a seat here for a minute if you’d be so kind.’’

Well, obviously something *had* come up, something to do with that businessman who’d gone in ahead of her. Eva was more than happy to wait, if she could just keep Fanny amused. The reception area was comfortably furnished with a settee and two chairs. There were original paintings on the walls and the gentle sounds of water running from a fountain, artfully designed into one corner of the waiting area. ‘‘Fanny? Come and look at the waterfall—’’

Too late. The girl had marched to the door the

businessman had disappeared into and opened it wide.

"Hi, Daddy! Guess what—hey, you got your *hair* cutted!"

CHAPTER TWENTY-FOUR

"*FANNY!*" Eva stared at the receptionist who gazed back, equally shocked.

"*Daddy?*" she whispered.

The two women moved as one to the open door.

Silas had scooped up Fanny, still carrying her shopping bag, and she was reaching up to feel his hair, oblivious to the rest of the people in the room. Silas set the girl down on the edge of his desk, keeping one arm protectively around her shoulders.

The man who'd opened the door for them stared at the girl, idly kicking her legs against the side of the desk. "This is *Fanny?*"

"Yep." Fanny nodded vigorously, looking into the shoe bag. "We were shopping for school stuff. We got lots. Do you want to see my new shoes, Dad?"

The black woman on the sofa let out a moan and leaned against the man beside her, who put his arms around her. "Hush, darling," he said in a low voice. "Everything's all right."

Vivian! It had to be. Eva knew immediately that the woman was Fanny's birth mother.

Silas looked stricken. The last person he'd expected to walk into this room, she realized, was his daughter.

She moved toward him, feeling as if she was stepping on oyster shells. ''Hello, Silas. Sorry we're a bit early,'' she said calmly. She turned to the visitors and smiled—and took a chance. ''You must be Vivian. I'm Eva Haines, Silas's fiancée. I'm so pleased to meet you.''

That broke the ice. Suddenly everyone was talking at once, everyone but the receptionist, who was clinging limply to the doorframe, still looking pale, and Fanny, who was trying on her new shoes, blissfully unaware of the charged atmosphere surrounding her.

The man who'd held the door for them turned out to be Scott Carradine, Silas's good friend and lawyer. All the adults involved seemed to grasp immediately, for the sake of the child present, that there could be no explanations or recriminations.

After a few minutes, Eva suggested she take Fanny on to the restaurant, as though that had been the plan all along, with Silas to join her later. The heartfelt look Vivian sent her as Eva gathered up Fanny's old shoes and stuffed them into the bag was all the thanks she needed. The poor woman! Vivian was trembling as she said goodbye to them. She suddenly knelt down and gave Fanny a hug, and Eva nearly cried when she saw the anguish in Silas's eyes. They were caught in the middle of an impossible situation, all of them.

"Bye!" Fanny waved cheerfully, oblivious to everything except the prospect of lunch with Eva and her father "in the restaurant in the sky" and the fact that she would be going to school in a few weeks. And, judging by the way Fanny was watching her feet as she walked, that she had new shoes.

That night, in bed, Silas told Eva the whole story. Scott had come to an agreement with Vivian and Armand that they would be able to get to know Fanny, but that Vivian would sign over custody to Silas. He wasn't sure how it would work—Scott was going to figure out the details—but Vivian would acknowledge Silas as Fanny's father and have Fanny's birth certificate changed. She'd also swear an affidavit as to the extraordinary circumstances, why she'd left Fanny, with whom she'd left her, how much money had changed hands, everything. Then Scott planned to try to swing a deal with the law, if it came to that. At present, they didn't even know if there was an open file on Fanny's abduction.

What a mess! Eva was just glad things had worked out the way they had. Her heart went out to Vivian, who had suffered so much, not only having to give up her baby in the first place but learning later that her child had disappeared.

Eva wasn't sure that, in Vivian's place, she'd have been as forgiving of Silas.

Still, the situation was on its way to being resolved, she hoped. Best of all, she had Silas. And Fanny. And, in time, another child or two. Nothing, not even the offer of a full-time job teaching in the school of her choice, could make her own prospects look any brighter.

"...AND THAT'S REALLY what was behind that old feud all these years."

"That my mother's cousin was in love with *your* grandfather?" Eva's voice was incredulous.

"More than that. They were having a hot and heavy affair for many years, apparently." Silas flipped the last of the burgers on the barbecue and adjusted the heat on the grill.

"An *affair?*" Aggie looked as astonished as Eva.

"Yes. An affair," Silas repeated with a smile. "You know, where a man and a woman—"

"I *know* what an affair is, young man," Aggie snapped, with a glance at Ivor, who was silently making his way through a plateful of potato salad before the burgers were served, and then at Fanny, who was swinging in the rope swing in the arbutus tree thirty feet away. They were celebrating Ivor's birthday. Matthew sat in a lawn chair, smoking his pipe and watching Fanny.

"Little pitchers have big ears," Aggie said meaningfully.

"But those big ears can't hear this far," he retorted mildly. "At any rate, Doris was in love with my grandfather and her own husband at the same time, or so she told me."

"Two men! That's what Doris said when I visited her. I didn't understand. I thought she meant she'd been in love with someone *before* Charles came along!" Eva said. "I had a totally different romantic picture figured out when she gave me that warning about loving two men at once."

Silas nodded. "Apparently, Charles had been in poor health for a while, which made her feel doubly guilty about carrying on an affair behind his back for all those years. With his best friend, at that. When he finally died, she fully expected to marry my grandfather, who'd been widowed for years, after a decent interval. According to Doris—and I saw the love letters so I have to agree with her—Hector had always promised to marry her. But when Charles died, my grandfather wasn't here. He'd gone off to Europe and—"

"Going off to Europe seems to be problematic for the men in your family," Eva interrupted. "I think we'd better not go to Europe anytime soon."

''As I was saying,'' Silas continued, smiling, ''off he went to Europe one winter, with my uncle Leo and my dad, who were just boys of about ten or twelve, and when he came back, he had a Swedish wife in tow. Birgit is my grandmother on two sides, really, since my mother's her daughter and my father's her stepson.'' He shook his head and started sliding burgers onto the platter in the warming tray. ''Do you follow all this, Eva? I can't blame you if you don't.''

Eva had been rapt while he'd recounted the story her cousin had told him in the lodge that afternoon. ''Doris never forgave him.''

''Never did. He'd ruined her prospects and her life, she said. He'd lied to her. After that, she told me she made up her mind that he was as good as dead, and she never spoke to him again. Or to anyone else in our family, for that matter. Crazy, isn't it?'' He didn't mention that Doris had also figured out that he'd had a hand in her rescue, because she knew very well that she never carried the cell phone Jack had insisted she own. That was a little secret between him and his cranky neighbor.

''Mmm. Was Hector the one who'd given her the garnet necklace?''

''Yes. And the music box. She did that hatchet job on the drawer herself, she told me, because she never wanted to see the letters or the box again but she couldn't bear to actually get rid of them."

"I can definitely understand that," Eva said dryly. "Doris didn't throw anything out."

Silas suddenly stood straight. "Did you hear that? It sounded like a chain saw."

"Probably across the water, on another island," Aggie said. "You know how sound travels."

"Perhaps." Silas put the burgers on the table. "Dinner is served."

"Yay!" Fanny ran to the table and sat down.

"You'd better go wash your hands, young lady," Aggie said, smiling as she watched the girl run into the house. "I won't be bossing her around much longer."

Aggie and Matthew were returning to their cottage at Hopkins Landing the following week. Silas and Eva and Fanny were moving to the condo, to get ready for life in the city again. Eva had a meeting the week after that to talk to a representative of the marine trust. Doris would be handing over title to her half of the island, as planned. Somewhere in there, they'd squeeze in a wedding.

"Daddy! Daddy!" Fanny burst out of the house and raced around the corner, toward the harbor. "Look! There's Sue Ellen and Monica!" She must have glimpsed them through the kitchen window.

"Sue Ellen!" Eva got up from her lawn chair and hurried after Fanny.

A few seconds later they returned, with the out-of-breath girls from Alberta, followed by the dachshund. Grandpa appeared to have run out of sunscreen, Silas observed, if the freckled cheeks and peeling noses of the two sunburned girls were any indication.

"Where's Grandpa?" Eva asked.

Sue Ellen eyed the cake on the table with interest. Ivor was still shoveling potato salad into his mouth. He hadn't missed a beat. "Oh, he's back on the other side. Grandpa and the old lady are burning down the house."

"Burning down the *house!* What are you *talking* about?" Eva's gaze sought his, and Silas's reaction was instantaneous: *And I thought* my *family was nuts.*

"Come on." He took Eva's hand and they ran toward the path that led to the eastern side of the island. Too late. By the time they got to the fork in the trail, they could see black smoke rising above the trees.

When they crossed the creek, the whole house was aflame. Doris was leaning on her cane, well away from the conflagration, shouting.

"Joy!" he heard her say, striking her cane on the ground.

"Joy!" Jack shouted.

"Grief!" she said.

"Grief!" Jack shouted, his fist in the air. *"Grief!"*

"Dad! Dad! Are you crazy? What are you and Doris doing?" Eva ran to her father and grabbed his arm.

"Too late, Eva. This house was a house of joy and sorrow. Dust to dust, ashes to ashes." Her father beamed at her. "It's best, honey. Doris wanted it gone. It's taken up too much of her life. Time to move on."

"Doris?"

"It's true, Eva," the old woman said. "Your father came to say goodbye, and I told him I had only two things I wanted to do. I wanted to see Andy again and I wanted to come back here once more. So he brought me."

Eva wheeled and Silas followed her gaze. There was the *Jack-in-the-Box,* tied up securely to the splintered wharf, next to the *Edie B.*

"Don't worry, Eva," Jack said, patting his daughter's hand. "I took precautions. I cut down those old trees next to the house so nothing else would catch. And—" he squinted up at the sky "—I can't feel a breath of wind. It won't spread."

There was nothing to do but stand there and watch the old house burn. Eva moved away from her father, and Silas put his arm around her and held her close.

"Have you two had dinner?" Jack Haines asked suddenly, including Silas in his query. "I've got some hot dogs on the boat although I believe—ha-ha—this might be a little hot for a wiener roast."

"We've got dinner on at the house. A barbecue. It's Ivor's birthday. Why don't you and Doris join us?" Silas said.

Doris fixed him with her pale icy gaze for a few seconds, putting him in mind of the legendary goats that supposedly inhabited Abel's Peak. Then she smiled. It was strange to see the old woman actually smiling, wintry though that smile was. "I believe I will," she said.

Silas offered his other arm and she took it. "Thank you, young man. It's been quite some time since I've been to that side of the island."

The three of them made their way to the creek, Silas and the two women, with Jack following.

"AND WHAT ABOUT you, Thomas? Can you tell us a little about your family?" Eva loved seeing who was in her new class. This fall, she had twenty-three students at Colonel Bingham Elementary in Vancouver's West End, not far from the condo.

"I've got a mom and a dad and a budgie bird," Thomas said, barely audible.

"Does your budgie have a name?"

The boy shook his head slowly and turned around to search for his mother in the small crowd of parents who sat on tiny kindergarten chairs at the back of the room. His mother, a redhead in jogging fleece, smiled encouragingly at her son.

"What color is he?"

"He's green and his name is Leaf."

"That's a nice name! Jennifer, can you tell us something about your family?"

Eva caught Silas's eye as the girl began to speak. He looked so proud and loving—the *perfect* father, attending his daughter's first day at school, like all the other moms and dads.

Eva was substituting for a teacher on maternity leave until Christmas. Perhaps by then, Eva thought with a skip in her heartbeat, she'd be planning maternity leave herself. She had her fingers crossed.

"How about you, Fanny? Can you stand up and tell us something about yourself?"

"Sure, I can." Fanny got to her feet, looking resplendent in her matching red plaid outfit, skirt, vest and blouse. Even her hair boasted a bright-red plaid ribbon. "I've got a dad and he's back there—" she pointed to Silas, who smiled "—and I've got *two* moms, one who lives in San Fran-cis-co, and a great big dog named Bruno and I have a squirrel—"

"A squirrel!" one boy burst out admiringly.

Fanny nodded. "Yep. His name is Kelly and I even know a donkey named Andy."

Eva watched the children's eyes widen as Fanny completed her litany. It was nearly time for the bell to ring.

"That was lovely, Fanny." The buzzer sounded and all the children looked at her. "We can take a break now, children. If you'd like a snack, you can get one at the back of the room and if you'd like to go to the washroom, you may go now."

The parents had brought snacks for the first day, and Eva saw everything on the table from sushi to celery sticks. As the parents moved forward to help their children orient themselves at their first recess on their first day of school, Eva felt Silas's arm steal around her waist. "Quite the girl, isn't she?" he whispered, dropping a kiss on the nape of her neck.

Eva nodded. "No kissing the teacher," she whispered back, blushing.

"Hey, we're still on our honeymoon!" They were married a week ago, in a private ceremony at City Hall, with Fanny, Scott, the Klassens, Eva's father and Silas's mother in attendance.

She smiled in response, glancing around the classroom.

"What do you think, Teacher? Have three years on Liberty Island set her back any?"

"Hardly," Eva replied. "Were you worried?"

''Not really. She's a survivor.'' Silas couldn't have sounded prouder.

Two girls, one Chinese and the other with blond braids, approached Fanny. ''I have a dog, too. Where's your dog?'' the one with braids asked.

''That's funny! He's at home. Dogs can't come to school, school's for *kids!*'' Fanny shot a glance toward her father and Eva and Eva smiled. Her classroom was a wonderful mix, with children from all kinds of backgrounds, even one little girl who'd shown up with two obviously very nervous dads.

''And no bringing Bruno to school for Show and Tell, either,'' she said. She could definitely see Fanny doing just that.

''Isn't this the child who tried to run away from home so she could go to school?'' Silas mused quietly.

''Your wild child.''

''*Our* wild child,'' he said, and kissed her ear again. ''The first, I hope, of many wild children.''

He moved off to deliver his contribution to the snack table.

''Cupcakes, anyone?'' he asked, presenting the paper bag from the Denman Street bakery.

''What kind, Dad?'' Fanny was holding hands with the two girls. They were already friends.

''Chocolate chip, I believe.'' Silas peered into the bag. ''With icing.''

"Yippee!" The girls reached for the bag and began sharing the cupcakes with the other children.

It didn't take long for kids to make friends, Silas thought. Not even a little wild girl from Liberty Island.